She Still Lives

D1113694

*S*HE
*S*TILL
*L*IVES

A Novel of Tibet

BILL MAGEE

Snow Lion Publications

Ithaca, New York
Boulder, Colorado

Snow Lion Publications
P.O. Box 6483
Ithaca, NY 14851 USA
(607) 273-8519
www.snowlionpub.com

Copyright © 2006 by Bill Magee
All rights reserved. No portions of this book may be reproduced
by any means without prior written permission from the publisher.

Printed in U.S.A. on acid-free recycled paper.

ISBN-10   1-55939-247-9
ISBN-13   978-1-55939-247-1

Library of Congress Cataloging-in Publication Data

Magee, William A.
    She still lives : a novel of Tibet / Bill Magee.
       p. cm.
    ISBN-13: 978-1-55939-247-1 (acid-free paper)
    ISBN-10: 1-55939-247-9 (acid-free paper)
    1. Tibet (China)—Fiction. 2. Liberty—Fiction. 3. Dalai lamas—
Fiction. 4. Political fiction.   I. Title.
PS3613.A3436S54 2006
813'.6--dc22
                                             2006020103

To the Memory of Stella

One must think like a hero
to behave like a merely
decent human being.
—May Sarton

1

Beijing Releases Five

Beijing, January 12, 2114 (Xinhua). Department of Public Security officials today announced plans to release five persons currently serving prison terms for their roles in the Tibetan nationalist uprising of 2099. Mila Lakpa, Puntsok Denpa, Jamyang Tashi, Basang Uri Garma, and Kunchok Gunru, all of New Tibet City, were convicted of conspiring with Tara Gyatso, the Seventeenth Dalai Lama, to create an independent Lamaist state. "The men will be released during the coming year," said Chu Si-Chuan, spokesman for the Department of Public Security. "However, there is no plan to release the Dalai Lama at this time. She is a long-time stubborn secessionist who has tried to split her Chinese motherland."

The prison doors opened reluctantly with the metallic grinding of a rusted vault. For a few seconds the narrow portal afforded an unsettling glimpse into the darkness of a maximum correctional facility. Then the gates clanged shut again—but not before Mila Lakpa stepped across the threshold to stand blinking and befuddled in the hard, bright sun.

A burly Tibetan fellow and his black retriever dog were waiting just down the hill. Seeing Mila, the man hailed him:

"Mila! *Ma peh!* Down here!"

Mila squinted at the owner of the voice. It was a voice to cause avalanches. He saw a big powerful man in mountain buckskins under a broad leather hat shading a ruddy face. Face and hat alike seemed smeared with grease and smoke. Mila hesitated for a second, his meager, undernourished form blending into the red blockhouse behind him. He looked around with an anxious glance—then stepped out briskly. Away, away at last from the hated walls; trotting pell-mell down the hill; gaining speed, a very little speed, and not without a creaking in the knees. He stumbled once or twice on the steep and rocky incline but managed to bring himself safely down from the prominence.

He was enveloped in a vast and odorous bear hug. A big red face filled all of Mila's vision. It was a rough face with uneven angles, like a deflated soccer ball kicked hard by a disappointed athlete, except that a large, happy, welcoming smile gleamed in the center of it: "Mila, do you still recognize me? I am Kunchok Gunru." The grip he had on Mila's arm was like a tourniquet.

Mila remembered.

"Gunru! I am honored that you have come to greet me."

"Let me be the first to congratulate you on surviving your, um, political eclipse, Mila."

"Thank you, it is good to be free, my old friend." Mila shaded his eyes and gazed up at the cloudless sky, the sun very near the zenith. "And to think it has been shining away up there all this time," he said. "My, my. No doubt we still have moon, stars, clouds—the whole thing?"

"The whole thing. Mila, this is my dog, Gochen."

Gochen was a glossy black hunter with a panting tongue and bright, attentive eyes. "What a winning pup you have here, Gunru!"

"You like her?"

"Most amazingly." said Mila. "She looks smart as paint. Is she yours?"

"Just temporarily. Gochen and I are heading up into the mountains." He clapped a friendly arm across Mila's shoulder. "Come, Su-su packed us both a lunch. We will go down to the village for our tea."

They began walking down a side road to the village, avoiding, as did all Tibetans, the main road to the prison.

"I did not recognize you at first, Gunru," admitted Mila. "When last I saw you, you were the aesthetic type. Now you look splendid, like a woodchopper."

"I was in the camps, Mila. Life in the camps is conducive to robust good health, or so we are told there. Take my arm. These rocks are loose footing for a jailbird."

"I am very glad you survived, Gunru. I feared we might never meet again."

"We have both survived, Mila." Gunru's sympathetic gaze roamed across his old friend. "But, to be truthful, you look like crap."

Mila knew that Gunru was referring to his shockingly starved condition, to his sparse, graying hair, his missing teeth, his flattened nose, and his stooped, shambling walk. Mila wanted to say something to ease his old friend's mind, but he could not find any light-hearted way to describe his fifteen years of beatings and deprivation—of maximum correction. How could he tell Gunru what was in his heart? How to express his gratitude that, after so many years of pacing alone around a dimly lit cage, he could now hold hard to Gunru's rock-steady biceps and proceed in a straight line? He possessed no words for that.

"Listen, Mila," said Gunru suddenly. "Su-su and I want to offer you a few days rest at her place until you are ready to move on again. What do you think?"

"I fear it will be dangerous for you."

"The police? I am afraid you are no longer deemed a threat to the State, my friend."

Mila looked mildly surprised. "Oh? In that case, I accept your kind invitation with pleasure."

"Good. Healthy food is what you need; lots of mountain air also."

The two men and the dog walked on. From time to time the hillside afforded them a fine view of the Tsur Valley. New Tibet City could be seen in the distance, nestled against the rugged mountains beyond it.

"I take it you have been out for a while, Gunru?"

"About two months."

"Have they been good months?"

"They have been mixed, I would say. But far better than being in the camps."

"What have you been doing?"

"I have been working with a surveying team in the mountains. This fortnight, I am taking some days off to help my sister in her fields. As you recall, she lives just a few hours' walk from here."

"And how is your dear sister?"

"She is well, thank you."

"Someone told me she was married," Mila said, looking at Gunru with a blank expression.

"Yes, but he is dead three years now."

"I am so sorry! How did it happen?"

"Land mine accident. Their place is not far from the mines. Su-su was injured too. She lost a foot."

"Dear lord! This is terrible news! Has she recuperated?"

"Oh, yes. She gets around quite well. Not like it used to be with her, of course. Quite a tragedy for a young woman. She has tough Gunru bones, though."

Mila shook his head. "I am appalled to hear of this. Poor Su-su! My heart goes out to her. Gunru, these land mines are our country's greatest evil."

"*Tagarang*. May they disappear from the land."

"I look forward to seeing your sister again, Gunru."

"Su-su looks forward to seeing you. She assures me your primary task will be consumption of lamb and noodle *tukpa*, but you are welcome to walk Gochen if you feel up to it."

"Do you know, I may be up to that," laughed Mila.

"Speaking of Gochen, are you enjoying her company so far, Mila?"

"Tremendously. A dog is a fine companion."

Gunru laughed. "Especially if the dog is like this one: a gene-spliced explosives sniffer."

"What, an alpha-sniffer? I have heard of them."

"The latest model. She is bred for enhanced empathic intuition. Gets right up into your head to see what's for dinner."

"Surely she is a fine animal. But, Gunru, why do you need such a beast?" Mila looked at his friend and his eyes narrowed suspiciously. "What exactly is it that you survey, Gunru?"

"I would not lie to you, Mila. But keep this to yourself. Last year the Chinese moved all their helicopters to Xinjiang. Some sort of trouble in the north. That means this year it has been possible for Tibetan patriots to survey clandestine routes over the mountains."

"Surveying in the mountains? Where, in the south?"

"Not the south, Mila, no."

"Surely not the north?"

"In fact, yes, the north. We are opening a safe route across the mountains into the Par Valley."

Mila looked puzzled. "Around the land mined areas?"

Gunru shook his head sadly. "There is no way around the mines, Mila. We go right into them. It is hazardous work, but it is important."

Mila drew a loud breath through the gaps in his teeth. He knew the area well from his childhood, when he had often hiked and climbed in the high mountains with his father. It was rugged Himalayan range and valley then. But now it was Tactical Area One, a military killing field so vast it sprawled across the mountains north and east of New Tibet City all the way to the garrison. It was said that a thousand thousand mines cursed that desolate terrain. The life of the rebellious city had withered in their punitive embrace, which had been its purpose from the beginning, of course.

"Isn't that rather dangerous work, Gunru?" was all Mila could say.

"No more dangerous than driving a truck, really."

"Nonsense. It is madness. Who employs you to do such a thing?"

"An unofficial guild of traders in New Tibet City."

"Smugglers, then?"

"To be sure."

"What sorts of goods?"

"All sorts, I suppose."

Mila shook his head in disbelief. "Tactical Area One!" He whistled his amazement and Gochen turned to regard him quizzically, her tongue exposed to the breeze. "It is the boneyard of all time. How do you keep your legs?—Of course: the dogs!"

Gunru's eyebrows rose beneath his hat brim. "Aye, it is possible to survey routes through the Tactical Area with an alpha-sniffer or two. Isn't science wonderful, Mila? I have a feeling that Gochen here is going to be a fine bomb spotter, aren't you girl?" Gochen wagged her fringed black tail. It sailed aloft like a little victory banner. "Gochen is a real prize. Did not cost us a single *song*. Some fellows we know liberated her from a security patrol. She sniffs everything, but explosives are her beat. Rather keen on cats, too, I find. If cats ever become a menace around here, we have us a hell of a defensive weapon. Did you ever hear of the Freetowners, Mila? Remember Jamyang? Jamyang Tashi? Our old comrade?"

"Jamyang Tashi?" Mila was having a memory lapse. "Indeed, it is a name to me."

"*Kay chay-gyi ma ray.*" Gunru looked sympathetically at his fuddled friend. "It doesn't matter, Mila."

They reached the bottom of the hill. The prison was high on top. It was good to be away from its ominous presence. Down below a small Tibetan village straddled the narrow road with houses clustered around a small bridge where a sparkling brook flowed to the river. It was all like a marvelous dream to Mila. Gunru took Mila's emaciated arm and steered him into an alley between two stone walls overgrown with vines. Soon they came to a secluded little temple to the goddess Tara, beside which an old woman tended a tea stall in a tiny grove of aspen and larch.

"Sit, Mila," said Gunru. They sat on benches. "Now we will eat and drink tea. How are you feeling?"

"I think I am all right."

"It takes some getting used to."

"I feel a little light-headed, but otherwise I am having fairly appropriate thoughts and feelings, I think."

Gunru laughed. "I would not bet on that. It takes quite a while. I still catch myself going crazy half the time. I dream about the camps at night and sometimes not at night, too."

"I am pained to hear that, old friend," said Mila, looking into Gunru's face with sudden concern.

The old woman brought tea.

"Here's to our freedom, Mila!" Gunru raised his teacup in a toast.

"To you, Gunru. It is good to be back." They drank tea. Mila savored the salty taste of it, almost—but not quite—forgotten.

Gunru pulled oiled-paper packages from his breast and gave one to Mila. "These are Su-su's pot stickers," he said. "Very tasty, I think you will agree."

Mila sat and regarded the delicious-smelling package of

dough and meat. A gift from a woman he knew long ago. He tried to concentrate on his sorrow for Su-su's dead husband and her own injury, but his mouth watered unashamedly. Mila gave in to his hunger. He said a small offering prayer and broke apart the somewhat squashed fried dumplings. He gave one to the dog, who gobbled the greasy morsel with pleasure. It felt good to have enough food to share with a friend. He tossed her another.

"Eat, Mila," chided Gunru. "You need your strength."

Mila sank his teeth into the pot stickers. Nothing so indescribably wonderful had ever entered his mouth. The spiced meat was juicy and flavored with onion. The dough was thick and chewy and fried in lard. He chewed and swallowed energetically, hearing himself growl a little as his teeth tore into the unfamiliar gristle. He drank another cup of tea, and the long-denied taste of butter and salt was unexpectedly poignant. He slowly closed his eyes. They remained closed until Gunru said:

"Are you troubled, Mila?"

Mila nodded. The trouble was, he had hundreds of memories of the Dalai Lama and he never knew which one might begin playing on the silver screen inside his head. Their value to his sanity varied. Sometimes she was Kundun in her ritual regalia, wielding vajra and bell. Now and then she appeared in his memories as Yishin Norbu, the wish-fulfilling jewel of the common people. Sometimes she was Her Holiness the Dharma Raja, chief adept of the Ganden practice lineage; or Tara Gyatso, media darling, accepting the Peace Prize from King Gustav Nineteen. Sometimes it was youthful Gyal-mo Rinpoche, Mila's Adolescent Goddess, walking barefoot in the daisies near the Summer Palace, popping grapes and licking her fingers as they debated the intricacies of Indian logic. One of Mila's favorite memories was of Musical Tara Gyatso in her private quarters, elegant in her Chinese robes amidst her fine collection of stringed instruments, indulging her passion for classical guitar. She adored the great players from years gone by: guitarists such as Manitas de Plata, Django Reinhart, Julian Bream, Jimi Hendrix, a special favorite she called *Gu-sha Jorpo*. . . . It seemed to Mila that he had infinite memories to draw upon, some of them inconsequential flashbacks; but others were poignant scenes from their long, sometimes ambiguous, always complicated friendship.

Now appearing on his inner screen was a familiar rerun. He might have called this bitter little short *Doomed Giaconda*. It starred Tara Gyatso in her flowing white satyagrahi robes, marching confidently to the summit of the Podrang Hill at the head of a long column of followers; her proud cheeks ruddy, dark eyes aflame, black hair blowing dramatically in the cold mountain wind. She was smiling enigmatically. Wasn't that the very last smile of their glorious dream together? It must nearly have been, for just then— or soon after—the tanks opened fire.

"Mila?"

Wresting his thoughts back to the present, Mila wanted to explain that he had eaten rich food too quickly, but his stomach both heaved and writhed. "Oh, blast," he said. Bile came into his throat. Before the horrified eyes of the tea stall woman, he puked over the wall.

"Happens to everyone the first time," said Gunru, nonchalantly lighting a small cigar with a wooden match. "'Take it slow, keep it down,' as we say in the camps. Water?"

Mila rinsed his mouth from the canteen. His poor head was swimming. He wiped his lips on the sleeve of the very tunic he had worn on entering prison. They had given it back to him, and it smelled of mold and mothballs and now vomit. It was also too large for his current form. The cuffs hung over his emaciated wrists as if his arms had somehow shrunk.

"You know something, Gunru-la," said Mila, after taking a few successful bites and passing another mouthful to the waiting dog: "Purely between us, I am not entirely surprised to hear that you have found illegal work in the minefields."

"No, Mila? Why is that?"

"I remember now what she used to call you."

"What? Pshaw! She never noticed me!"

"She did. She called you Jamgon, the protector of the earth, don't you remember?"

"She did?" Gunru beamed happily. "Be damned. I had no idea."

"And here you are, protecting the earth by de-mining."

Gunru considered that a moment. "But we are not really de-mining," he protested modestly. "Only surveying a clear trail."

"A paltry distinction. Tell me frankly, Gunru. How dangerous is it, in your honest opinion?"

Gunru had been asking himself this question for weeks. Survival in his outfit was not a given. He had already seen one sequence of events lead to disaster. The problem area had been an innocent-looking dip in the ridgeline. But the dogs had been over one particular part of it several times. They could not point to any mines but they were obviously nervous about the area; so naturally the men who walked behind them were nervous too. They were still learning, and learning fast, but one thing they had learned was that there were many ways to disguise the chemical signature of plastique: gasoline, bleach, pepper gas, bear shit. Sometimes the Chinese pulled such stunts, but not often. It was decided to give the area another sweep. The maps were laid out. The dogs were ready. The point man of Team A started his dog into the disputed area, but his angle of entry was too sharp and soon he was off the surveyed line. A nervous surveyor shouted a warning. This he should not have done: the well-trained sniffer-dog froze in her tracks. Then the point man turned his head to look back at his crew chief. This was a fatal mistake: the point man takes his eyes off the dog at his peril. Just at that moment the animal began to bay: an urgent head-back howling, and it was suddenly obvious to everyone that this field was littered with scent-doctored explosives, but the knowledge came too late. Stumbling forward over the hindquarters of his immobile hound, the point man gave out a wordless shout and slid sideways off her left flank, falling stiffly to the ground. Later, the consensus of the men was that the point man was basically at fault, but he had redeemed his mistake by shielding the dog's body with his own as the mine went off, cutting him almost in two but leaving her unharmed.

Thinking about it now, Gunru removed his hat and wiped the sweat from his brow.

"Are you ill, Gunru?" Mila asked.

Gunru shook his head. Ill was not what he was, exactly. Oppressed in dread; haunted by fearsome thoughts; determined to be brave; terrified even in sleep. In his ears he heard the anguished howling of the dog, crouched motionless amidst the billowing smoke. He heard the point man screaming: his intestines ablaze with a weird sputtering flame like a fire sacrifice. The acrid smoke reminded them all nauseatingly of *lo sar*, the new year celebration. The eyes of all the men were focused on Gunru. Why? It took Gunru a moment to remember that he carried the rifle.

They called it mountain triage: one shot in the head in payment for all your brave deeds. Gunru did the job. There was no hope for the point man, after all. Gunru did not feel particularly bad about it until later. There was not a man among them, including the point man, who did not want it to stop. Then at last, with the point man finally quiet, the dog stopped howling too. She lay still, panting. She was a real professional; a long-haired Tibetan mastiff trained by Nepali border guards; purchased, not stolen. A classic mountain beauty, although her muzzle was artificially widened to accommodate the sniffing gear. It was said she could smell every bear in Tibet. She seemed quite crestfallen, now. An agonizing hour passed while the crew discussed the possibility of a rescue.

Gunru stood a little apart from the discussion; the rifle he was holding was a terrible burden but he was afraid to give in to the impulse to drop it. He squeezed the handgrip until his knuckles were white. The poor dog waited patiently, whining under her breath. She knew her chances were slim. She looked at Gunru from time to time: he would be the one. The crew was strongly motivated to attempt a rescue, because the dog was crucial to the success of the survey in general and in particular because of her hard-earned knowledge of this ground. She was a great dog, and they almost decided to make the attempt; but in the end they did not. They turned to the man with the rifle. Gunru sweated. In a way it was just a dog; but in another way it was more difficult than the point man. In the end he had to hand off the rifle to the crew chief. No one said anything about it. But Gunru took it hard.

Mila was alarmed for his pale, perspiring, fear-haunted friend. "Gunru," he said, "Why not quit this frightening job? Surely your sister needs you on the farm. Can't you live the quiet life?"

"I am considering that. Although truthfully, it is hard to contemplate a quiet life under Communist rule."

"You have earned it."

"Through failure? I don't think so."

"Think of it as an extended holiday. Su-su would be delighted, isn't it so?"

"She says. And for her sake I am mulling it over. But first I must take Gochen up to her outfit."

"You cannot conceal your own fears, yet you are going to take this trusting pooch into the Tactical Area," said Mila with mild reproof.

Gunru gave Mila a sharp glance. "Certainly. Why not? She is needed there. She will be very well taken care of, you can be sure."

"Who was that fellow again? The Freeloader?"

"Freetowner. He is Jamyang Tashi."

"Oh, yes. Jamyang Tashi," said Mila. "Sure, I remember him now: Jamyang Tashi led one of the cohorts up the hill."

"That's him."

"And Jamyang is with the Freetowners?"

"Mayor of the place, he tells me."

"Guerilla bands liberate dogs now?"

"They do when the dogs are cutting edge explosive sniffers."

"How do they get the dogs away from the troops?"

"They kill the goddamned troops, Mila, what do you think?" snarled Gunru angrily.

Mila frowned. "Jamyang used to be a proponent of nonviolence," he said. "But I suppose times have changed."

Gunru snorted. "Jamyang was never a proponent of nonviolence, Mila. He was always a proponent of Jamyang."

"What about you, Gunru? Do you still renounce violence?"

Gunru's mind flashed again to the lesson he had learned about himself: he could shoot the point man but he could not shoot the point man's dog. So how the hell did that relate to renouncing violence? He scowled angrily into his cigar smoke.

"You know what, Mila? The Seventeenth used to ask people that same question. I thought it was damned irritating even coming from her. I mean, does the question have the slightest meaning? It's insulting."

"Nonviolence is insulting?" Mila again looked puzzled.

"It is not so cut-and-dried as the two of you were always telling us to think. I'll tell you something. I was offered a spot with the Freetowners last week, when Jamyang brought me the dog. A share of the take."

"A spot?"

"You know, a job. But I turned them down."

"Because they use violent means?"

Gunru's anger was gone, replaced by a sudden protectiveness

for his naive friend. He placed his large arm affectionately over Mila's shoulders. "You are a decent fellow, Mila," he said. "My sister says that in any other country you would be a bloody hero. But you are a little out of touch with the reality in Tibet. Let's just say the Dalai Lama has been gone a long time: maybe the people have forgotten."

"I have not forgotten. Have you forgotten, Gunru?"

Gunru considered. "Just a little," he admitted.

Mila shrugged. "I seriously doubt that."

Gunru sighed and hoisted his large body to its feet. He slapped some coins on the table. "Come, Mila, are you fully recovered? Let us continue on to Su-su's charming, restful farm."

"By all means, brother. Lead the way."

Gunru took Mila's arm in his protective grasp.

"Off we go, easy does it," he said. "Two old-timers and a dog; no danger to the State."

"That remains to be seen," sniffed Mila.

"Oho!" laughed Gunru with pleasure. "They have not kicked all of the spirit out of you yet, firebrand!"

"A man's courage does not reside in his balls," said Mila, quoting a prison proverb.

The trio walked on through a rolling yellow landscape down a road that led ever closer to Tactical Area One.

2

Gunru's sister's real name was Sukyi. She had lived alone these three years, since the land mine suddenly killed her husband while biting off the end of her foot. She was very fond of her brother and his visits were a great comfort to her. Although it sometimes seemed that his massive bulk would burst out the walls of her cozy front room, he kindly sat with her, hour after hour, gazing at fading photographs of their childhood. Seeing him coming down the road now, with their old friend Mila Lakpa, her heart rose in her chest. She put down the knitting and stood without her crutches at the front door of the little house.

"Gunru!"

"Su-su!" He came bounding up the steps to lift her in his embrace. Gochen raced past him into the house.

"Welcome home!"

"It is good to be back. Look here, I found Mila."

Gunru released her with a fond kiss and stepped aside. There was Mila, stepping shyly over the threshold into the warmly lit interior.

She had wanted to say, "You have not changed," and give him a quick kiss; but that was not possible. He was a shockingly different man. She would not have known him if she had seen him in the fields. His once black hair was sparse and graying; his nose was crooked. His brows were thickened with scar tissue, like a boxer's. He gave her a tentative smile that showed sorrowful gaps in his teeth.

"Hello, Sukyi," he said quietly.

"Oh, Mila." She threw her arms around him and held him close to her. She could feel his shoulder blades through his thin coat. His arms went around her and squeezed briefly.

She held him at arm's length and looked into his face. His eyes were the same: two pale gray reminders that Mila's grandfather had been an Australian adventurer. But the skin of his face was stretched tight across the skeletal cheeks and the bridge of his nose and his gray eyes were sunken into dark wells of exhaustion and pain.

"No need to cry," he assured her. "I am fine."

"You are starved," she said primly, wiping her eyes. "And I am only crying because you smell like a goat. Come in. I will take your coat. You will eat and bathe before you sleep. Oh, Mila. You poor thing. But after a few bowls of *tukpa* you will feel better. Then you may sleep. Sleep a week, if you wish."

She realized she was babbling, but could not stop herself. Mila, with a word of thanks for her kindness, entered and removed his shoes. Sukyi, limping slowly, seated Mila in her husband's old chair. Seeing the sad condition of his stockings, Sukyi sent her brother for hot water and woolen socks. She threw his old ones into the rag bin and knelt before him with a basin of water to bathe his feet. The look on Mila's face was one of pained embarrassment, but he let her guide his feet into the basin.

"Hot water!" he cried with amazement, looking around at Gunru as if to alert him to this wonderful thing.

But Gunru was looking at Mila's feet. Sukyi looked up and met her brother's glance.

"What's this, Mila?"

Mila was slumped back in his chair, smiling with pleasure as the hot water eased the various aches and pains in his feet and ankles.

"It has been a long time since I had hot feet," smiled Mila, ignoring the question. "Although I have been in hot water quite a bit." He tried to chuckle, but only a pathetic creaking sound came out of his chest.

"What did they do to you?" Gunru demanded.

Mila looked up at Gunru's angry scowl. "It is all right, Gunru," he said soothingly. "I tell you truthfully, it was so long ago that I have forgotten. I think it was no one thing. Toes are very vulnerable bits. They break readily; they get poor circulation; they succumb to frostbite"—and rat bites, but Mila would say nothing about the rats—"It's behind me. Forgotten. It's not serious . . . compared to some wounds." He squeezed Sukyi's shoulder.

"Oh, Mila."

"And it was long, long ago. At the beginning."

Mila lifted his feet from the cooling water and Sukyi toweled them dry. She slid thick woolen socks onto his damaged feet.

They ate meaty *tukpa* and yellow *dal* at a round oaken table before a cozy fire (Mila needed more warmth than the Gunrus). Gochen lay before the fire, happily sleeping; her own dinner of mutton bones cleaned and chewed. On the table were dishes of rice and greens, plates of okra with sliced mushrooms and garlic, cucumber pickles, pickled bamboo shoots in soy sauce, lotus root with ginger, and lovely colorful piles of mangoes, apples, and bananas. Mila ate ravenously, with the table manners of a youthful hyena, smiling all the while as if remembering something pleasant from very long ago. He ate all that was put before him and licked the plates. The *tukpa* was especially warming and delicious. A feeling of great well-being filled Mila. He looked with fondness at the craggy features of Gunru and the long, lovely face of his sister, now looking back at him with a tender expression, her black eyes gleaming in the yellow firelight.

Sukyi prepared a dish of mangoes while Gunru placed a ceramic bottle of *arak* and three small cups on the table. Gunru poured glasses of the fiery liquid, a hairy liquor of mare's milk, scraped drop by drop from horse blankets slung above wooden fermenting vats.

"Let us drink a toast, Mila. To old friends, reunited."

Mila drank the liquor, shuddering as the unfamiliar burning heat spread through his limbs. Yet after it subsided he felt even more comfortable. He was about to propose an unwise toast when Gochen started up from the hearth with a snort and a growl.

"What is it, girl? What do you smell?"

"Kunchok, I forgot to tell you. There was a police patrol on the road earlier this afternoon," said Sukyi, with an anxious look at her brother. "I saw them from the field. But they went away."

"I will check the road. Come, Gochen!" Gunru took a rifle from over the mantle. His boots resounded in the hall. The door slammed. Mila and Sukyi sat looking at each other in the sudden silence. Their hands came together as if by instinct.

"Oh, Mila. I missed you so much," Sukyi said. She leaned forward and pressed her lips to his. Her black hair fell around their shoulders. Mila's nose filled with the perfume of Sukyi's imported lilac soap. He had not forgotten it. Once upon a time he had brought her a small woven basket of soap from Beijing (the empty basket now held Sukyi's knitting).

Mila kissed her gently on the cheek and pulled his head out of the deliciously scented curtain of hair while he was still able. He wanted to look into her eyes and stroke her hair and cheek.

"I missed you. I missed you, Sukyi," Mila said truthfully. "Gunru tells me you lost your husband. I am so sorry. And you were injured." He stroked her cheek, smoothing the wet skin beneath her eyes. "You have suffered so much. I am sorry for you."

"He was a good man, Mila. You would have liked him."

"Tell me about him."

"He was a patriot. An intellectual and a farmer. In his youth he was arrested for writing revolutionary poetry. He went to prison. He married me. He died." She laughed a little. "He was a typical Tibetan."

"I'm sorry you lost him. I'm glad about the part where he married you, though."

"Thank you, Mila."

"You don't have to tell me anything else."

"Maybe not right now."

"I wanted you to be happy."

"I have loved some fine men, Mila." Her tears were falling silently onto the table, darkening the yellow grain of the oak.

"I know, I know," he said soothingly.

"But they just sort of . . . vanish."

"Dearest Sukyi . . ."

Her regularly composed features collapsed into a sad, wet contortion:

"I try so hard not to be jealous," she cried.

"I tried to warn you," Mila began hesitantly.

"Warn me?" She glared at him. "What woman wants a warning? And who would need one? Do you think we don't know the effect she has on you men?"

"She has an effect on everyone."

"What about me? Do you think I like being the first woman in history to lose her man to the Dalai Lama?"

"Now Sukyi, I wouldn't characterize it that way."

"Oh, you wouldn't? Maybe I was not the first after all?"

Mila said nothing. This angered Sukyi further.

"I don't blame her, Mila. You were such a handsome man once!"

She saw the look on Mila's face. Suddenly her anger drained away.

"Mila, I am sorry. I did not mean to hurt you."

Just then boots and paws were heard on the steps. Mila and Sukyi separated with a guilty look. Sukyi wiped her eyes with a cotton napkin. Gunru and Gochen burst into the room, bringing with them an unseasonable chilly wind.

"Something out there," said Gunru. "Not sure what. Gochen chased it off. Perhaps a wolf."

"I wish I had remembered to tell you about the police patrol."

"They were not looking for me, or they would have come up the path."

"I recognized some of the faces of the village militia."

"Those country fellows? Nothing to worry about." Gunru resumed his seat at the head of the table. He looked at Sukyi and then at Mila.

A silence settled over the house, disturbed only by Gochen lapping water.

"I have interrupted a conversation," he said flatly.

Sukyi placed a hand on his arm. "We are catching up on lost years, dear brother. I am so happy that our Mila has returned to us."

"This was the best meal I have ever eaten," said Mila, belching politely and bowing to his hosts. "Now I must wash and sleep, hopefully in that order."

"I have hot water waiting for you, Mila. Gunru, warm his sheets."

Gunru growled, but he rose obediently to do his sibling's bidding.

That night Mila slept in a feather bed for the first time in his life. He was not entirely comfortable in its yielding embrace. Towards morning he had a dream in which he sailed a small round boat across a troubled ocean. Mila had never seen an ocean, except in his dreams. Its depths were deep purple, marbled with streams of bright green. Its surface was flecked with gold bubbles.

Each bubble was a water moon. The ocean heaved incessantly, and Mila believed it was pushed up from below by volcanic pressure. Rainbow-colored fish sailed above the waves. Far off, beyond his line of sight, sirens sang on a tropical shore. Glaciers sailed on the far horizon. In the near distance, a leviathan surfaced and spouted, sounding with a smack of its rubbery tail. The towering waves scraped their foaming white tops against the violent thunderheads, sparking silent fangs of lightning. Sea and sky were one color, connected at intervals by waterspouts that corkscrewed up from the ocean bed to bell their throats into cloud. Sea and sky were one element: no mariner could tell cloud from water. From Mila's viewpoint, the sea was crowded with bizarre, misbegotten craft. Brave sailors maneuvered around the spouts, voyaging across the sea in multi-decked leather and steel boats. Whalers sought their fishy prey in giant iron pots. The pots were hot. Steaming blubber rendered into oil propelled the diesel-powered oars. The harpooners flung their barbed shafts left and right at walruses, porpoises, nagas, dolphins, swordfish, and at the sharks that came in echelons to attack the numerous fish that swam in endless circles around each coracle. This was the setting of Mila's dream, and for what seemed like a long time he tossed helplessly on the violent, colorful, heaving sea; stuck corklike in the coracle; always moving on foamy wave tops beneath violently churning clouds.

Then a single ray of sunlight broke through the clouds, illuminating a purple circle of ocean not far away. To his surprise and growing excitement, he espied the Dalai Lama, garbed in white, in her own little boat, strumming a guitar and singing a mournful tune; mournful, but as youthful and vivid as the last time Mila had seen her, five thousand five hundred days ago.

Mila shipped his oars and rowed furiously across the heaving purple waves, but the harder he rowed, the less forward progress he made until, finally, she was just a speck on a turbulent sea where a stray beam of sunlight picked out the flash of her arms, strumming, strumming. He could barely hear the words of her song, a sentimental favorite from long ago:

> *Remnants of the love we pledged together,*
> *Remnants of the future that we planned,*
> *Remnants of the one I'll love forever,*
> *Remnants of a merely decent man . . . "*

Then she was out of sight beyond the waves. He awoke with light in his eyes and his first thought was: *I am in Narkang Prison.* Then he remembered. He was free. He threw back the covers and stood shivering on the cold boards. He dressed in clothing Sukyi had laid out for him the night before. Her dead husband's clothes: a loose fit.

Sukyi's small house was silent. The polished handmade furniture glowed yellow. A note on the table bade him good morning in Sukyi's flowing script. They had gone with Gochen to the village to purchase supplies. There was breakfast on the table.

Mila ate quickly—oat porridge with dried fruit and pig ear *mo-mo*. Coffee! He washed his bowls in the stone basin. Then he laced his new boots and went outside. It was warmer out of doors. The air was fresh and cool. He visited the outhouse: he had almost forgotten the feeling of privacy. Buckling his trousers, he strolled through the green garden. Sukyi's house and onion field lay between two steep hills. The hill to the east was not wooded, but was covered with pale gorse. To the west was a wooded hill with steep bluffs, jutting with stone. Before him was the road downhill to the village.

Mila intended to follow his friends' steps into town, but the thought of a pleasant stroll on a wooded hillside took him to the west.

Mila walked through the conifer forest. Perhaps because of his good boots, his feet and knees felt more supple than they had in years. They carried him up to an outcropping of rock. He stood in the sunlight looking over Tsur Valley to a long line of mountains.

Clouds shaded their southern face, making the normally sparkling peaks look black and ominous. Mila peered at them. Those peaks were the geographical center of Tactical Area One. Beyond them lay the Par Valley.

Mila closed his eyes. Something was tugging at his mind. Oddly, as if by instinct, he began sniffing the wind. His own normally poor sense of smell was quickly overwhelmed by a startling influx, an olfactory orchestra of the impressions of various odors. They increased in power until they utterly filled the dome inside his head. Each pungent odor was far more vivid and powerful than anything he had ever smelled in his life. His nose—no, not his nose, not precisely, but *something* in Mila's face—was alive with a spectrum of odors: the narcotic sweetness of madragon flower, the raw meat of a large mammal torn apart by a panther, the ghastly reek off the slick haunches of a love-struck bear. His new sense of smell was wonderfully directional—just up *there* in the hills.

Mila reeled. The palette of odors presented to his mind was too rich and complex, the input too strong for his physical mechanisms. He gagged; his eyes watered; he staggered blindly, not in pain exactly: overwhelmed. He pressed his hands over his nose, but the rancid smell of his own skin was no improvement.

With effort, Mila found he was able to banish certain odors one by one to the rear of his sinuses. He dismissed the delicious sharp pine scent, the pure smell of clean air moving over wet rock, the sulphurous gloom of a *wen chuan*. Then he could smell what was left quite clearly, underlying all other impressions: the sharp chemical whiff of plastique, collected from a thousand deadly sources and carried on the wind. It held his attention. He could not at this distance make out individual land mines, but from the pattern of the smell he could tell that the explosives lay everywhere—thousands and thousands of them in randomized patterns buried among the pine, larch, aspen, spruce, and on the upper slopes beneath rock and snow.

Now he was becoming accustomed to his heightened canine awareness. He realized he was sifting in detail through Gochen's nasal impressions. There was the sweat and leather marking Gunru's position; there, the flowery, delicate presence of Sukyi, slightly marred by the dank odor of a leg of mutton she must have purchased at the market.

Mila strove for a complete picture of Gochen's surroundings. He was not happy about a new set of smells that had arrived on the scene: diesel fumes, leather boots, beery breath, stale tobacco smoke, the uneasy sweat of fear. Then a sharper edge to the fear, coming strongly from Gunru, less noticeable through the scent of lilac soap on the woman he once knew so well, standing beside her brother's buckskin and gun oil. Fear on the air from unknown persons. Then the sudden, sharp tang of mortal terror. Then nothing.

Mila's connection to Gochen ended. The grand accumulation of odors that informed him of Gochen's world was over as suddenly as it had begun. Mila stood trembling on the outcropping of rock, searching his mind for the door back to that world of odors, back to Gochen's nose.

Was he going insane? Or had he somehow broken through to the dog's sense of smell? Could he have imagined it? Mila wondered. Can a man imagine shapes and colors other than those he has always known? Even now, the memory receded from his mind. He could no longer reconcile his powerful sensory experience with the pitiful, weak impressions now stirring his human nose.

Mila remembered the strange thing Gunru had said about the dog: *She is bred for enhanced empathic intuition.* At the time he had dismissed it as a joke. But now Mila felt a rising unease. *Enhanced empathic intuition?* Perhaps it was true: science had no doubt made many advances during his time in prison. Mila had been told that he himself possessed considerable intuition. Could it be possible? It must be true. Mila and the dog had achieved a telepathic nose consciousness, surely one of the most unheralded of yogic states.

Well-documented or not, Mila believed he had experienced it. He had smelled their surroundings; he had smelled his friends' fear. He turned and retraced his steps rapidly back down the mountain. When he reached the road to the village he began to run. His boots raised puffs of dust. His heart was pounding and his breath burning in his chest by the time he came upon the scene.

Gochen's dead body lay amongst the weeds on the side of the rutted roadway. Mila knelt beside her and stroked her black fur. His hand came up wet with blood, and he knew she had been shot through the chest. He ground the dust of the road between his palms to remove the red blood. He stood and surveyed the marks of the crime. Here to the east lay the tracks of a heavy vehicle backing into the verge; and there lay the leg of mutton, spilling redly out of its butcher paper.

Mila took of his coat and wrapped the dog's carcass in it. She was not a very large dog, but for Mila she was heavy. He carried her still-warm body into the village.

The village was built along just the one road. There were no side streets. A mountain stream ran beside the village. The streambed was steep and stony. Upthrust rocks pushed back shining heads of green-tinted water.

An official van sat unguarded outside the Police Station. Mila touched its bonnet. Its engine was still warm.

Mila went up the steps past the red stars of the People's Republic and entered the Police Station. Two bored Chinese policemen looked him over as stepped up to the divider. It was obvious to them that he was a jailbird, but the sight was so common as to arouse no suspicion. They must have thought Mila's bundled coat was his marketing. But they put their hands to their holsters when Mila marched boldly to the sergeant's station and dumped the dead beast unceremoniously on his desk.

"What the hell is this?" the sergeant cried, leaping to his feet.

"Your men have arrested my friends and murdered this dog," said Mila, his voice trembling with rage.

The two policemen behind him laughed, and the sergeant relaxed and resumed his seat.

"Oh, so that's it? Murdering dogs is a dire offense. And what is your name, my angry friend? You say Lakpa?" He consulted his ledger. "We do not want you, old-timer," he said to Mila with bored contempt. "You may go."

At this point, prudence would have dictated that Mila leave. But Mila was too angry.

"I want to see someone in authority. I want to see a lawyer for the people. I demand to see my friends. I want to lodge a strong complaint about the shooting of the dog." Mila was practically vibrating with rage.

"Throw him out," said the sergeant to the two officers. "The next time they see you, old Lakpa, they will shoot you dead."

The two guards picked Mila up like a sack of flour. As he hung in their strong grip above the scuffed and dirty wooden floor, he uttered one sharp cry: a cry of fury, total loss, and bitterness; then they banged the station door with his head and heaved him with a grunt clear out of the station. The carcass of the dog soon followed, still half-covered by Mila's overcoat.

All was quiet on the town's only street.

After a short time Mila picked himself up, re-wrapped Gochen, and hobbled painfully away with her.

Not far from the police station, an old man leaned out of a doorway and beckoned Mila inside. Mila followed the old man's crooked gait into a storage room with a rusty bicycle and a gardener's clutter. They passed through to a squalid kitchen smelling of rancid oil and chilies. The sound of running water was loud out the back window.

Following the old man's gestures, Mila placed the dog on the kitchen table. The old man unwrapped it and gave its wound a studied glance.

"All right," he said. "It was shot clean through. Nothing to be done about it. If you like, we can take him up the hill to the *chorten* near the old *gompa*."

Mila nodded grimly.

"Here now, I know you," the old man said hoarsely. "You are that sly one, Lakpa. What in the name of Tara Gyatso was you wanting in a Police Station?"

"Old man," said Mila, rubbing the back of his neck and grimacing. "They have arrested my friends and killed this dog."

The old man produced a yellow package of Chinese cigarettes.

"Smoke?"

"No thanks."

"They brought your friends in about an hour ago," said the old man, lighting a kitchen match on the side of a rusty tin of *cha*. "I know them folks. I seen them often. Nice couple, too. They live up over the hill, above Tsur Valley. Now that I see you two is friends, I reckon he must be Gunru—unless he is Puntsok Denpa?"

"He is Gunru. And his sister Sukyi."

"Got them for illegal trespass in the mountains, as I heard it. Got that from Lao Liao, who sweeps the exercise yard."

"Sweet goddess," prayed Mila, his breath leaving his lungs with a tired, defeated sigh. His rage at the arrest and shooting left him, to be replaced by a dull horror at his friends' fate.

"You all right, feller? They gave you a good toss, a damned good toss. Maybe a record throw."

"Right on my neck," said Mila ruefully, wincing with pain.

"What did they tell you about your friends?"

"Nothing. The communication was mainly about being shot on sight."

"Oh, they will, too. Shoot you on sight. Why the hell not? Bloody bastards. They do it all the time. Look, look there across the street, they are out already, just looking for you." The man pulled Mila deeper into his kitchen. "Tell you what to do. Leave the dog with me. I'll take him up the hill in the dark. You go out here. Cross the stream. Go straight out of town south over that hill. Take you right to New Tibet City. Don't go west. Remember: don't go west. And take this coat. It was my wife's. There. Looks good on you. Long life to her!"

He held out his hand. Mila gripped it in thanks, but his heart was too bitter to reply. He turned to go.

"Wait, wait. I want to hear you say it. It will be good luck, coming from you. Say it!"

Mila turned back. His sight seemed to clear. For the first time he noticed the scars that dented the old man's high, round cheekbones. The old man smiled. His teeth were ill-fitting Chinese-made dentures. He had been inside.

So Mila completed the prison formula: "She still lives," he said, hoping it was true.

3

New Tibet City was as much a warning against Tibetan nationalism as it was a functioning city. Its cratered streets and blasted monuments spoke eloquently of that day in 2099 when the Army opened fire on the independence movement. The city was not entirely dead, of course. The littered alleys were still packed with outdoor stalls, their cart wheels sheltering flea-ridden dogs and scrawny cats. The shops and unlicensed markets in the center of town were crowded with elderly Tibetan ladies, window-shopping lamas, school children, soldiers with red stars on their caps, mothers with string bags of green stuff, Hong Kong tourists photographing the Podrang, Mongolian engineers touring the Highway of Tunnels, and many others. But the old quarter was mainly rubble: tent cities had grown up like mushroom colonies partially sheltered by ragged, bullet-scarred walls. Blowing sand had softened the edges of the blasted stone.

The tent city where Mila lived included a mixed group of inhabitants: ex-politicals, criminals of various sorts, defrocked lamas, bankrupt merchants, hunted lawyers, human remnants from the camps, and so forth. It was not a place where the tourists lingered.

There were many unoccupied tents, but Mila felt lucky to find this one. It was comfortably situated between the remains of two old houses. Beside the tent was a garden. The tent's actual owners had kept pigs and vanished one night without a word to anyone, except presumably the pigs. The lady who owned the garden told Mila that she would only charge him an initial payment of fifteen *song*. "What for?" asked Mila. "Why should I pay you fifteen *song* when you do not own the tent and I do not live in your garden?" "Ah," said the woman. "But I own the garden gate, which you see hanging from its hinges there. Through that garden gate you have a view of the old Podrang Palace, standing in ruins atop the next hill. I can tell you are a patriot. In fact, you are Mila Lakpa. You have been in prison. Surely that view is worth fifteen *song* to a patriot just out of prison? Especially you. Or would you rather I ask my husband to put up the gate and you may keep your fifteen *song*?"

Mila decided it was worth fifteen *song*. He brought his belongings into the tent and found it soaked in pig grease and blackened with smoke. Small vermin infested the canvas side-cloths and the corners stank of pig shit. Sanitation was by way of a public latrine down a cobbled street: an open stage slung over running water. Cooking water came from upstream, although upstream is always downstream from somewhere in New Tibet City. But for Mila Lakpa it was a step up in his living arrangements, however he considered it.

Partly in memory of Sukyi and Gunru, Mila borrowed some tools from a childhood friend and went into business making wooden legs and crutches. There was constant need for both, due to the city's proximity to the Tactical Area. This melancholy livelihood both reflected and reinforced Mila's current somber worldview. To offer a clumsy wooden peg as the only compensation for the painful loss of a living leg—could there be a more fitting metaphor for the life they all were living? Sometimes, thinking of Sukyi and Gunru, Mila wondered about life and loss. Were they coextensive, mutually inclusive, synonymous, possessed of the same meaning? Or were they just the same damned thing?

In the evening he ate rice on a small stool under his opened tent flap overlooking the ruined Podrang. If the weather was fine, the sun would be going down and bands of purple would stretch from west to east. Sometimes he invited his neighbors on either side, Ding and Jamspel, to join him for dinner. They were not a congenial trio. Mila conceded that he himself was far from good mental health, after fifty-five hundred days and nights of prison; and Ding, who had been on a starvation-farm, sobbed whenever he saw a full bowl of rice. Even so, they were both doing better than Jamspel, who had been put back together carelessly after being taken apart by jointed truncheons in the camps.

Then the sun would set, and a canopy of stars would appear above the Tsur Valley. It was a scene of peace, but Mila's thoughts did not match it.

At night he slept very little. He sat alone in the dark, troubled by his thoughts, playing his old memories, waiting for dawn's first light.

On this particular day, dawn seemed slow in coming. Dawn meant the lifting of curfew, a time when Mila and his neighbors could safely go to the latrines. Waiting for dawn was always the hardest time. Sometimes he ignored the curfew and visited the latrines by the light of the stars—much of his political career had been conducted in the dark—but today it would be dangerous. Today was the fifteenth anniversary of the Freedom March.

Mila sat in the dark just inside his tent, thinking of that day, fifteen years ago. It had been the last day of Mila's youth. So many years separated him from that day, but he remembered the warm late summer breeze, the high, fleecy clouds, and the beautiful young Dalai Lama in her white satyagrahi robes, together with thousands of others all cloaked in white. The robes were entirely

Tara's idea. Mila wore them feeling like a damn fool. He told Tara the robes were bad luck—would infuriate the Chinese, assist with their targeting—and that is just what happened, in the swirling gas and raging fires: the once holy city swarming with armored vehicles; the Podrang Palace itself targeted from tanks on the flanking hills; white robes strewn throughout the rubble, stained red, injured bodies staining the cobbles.

When dawn spread its violet light through the encampment, Mila went to the latrine. His balls ached sometimes from being the sport of booted interrogators, and his bladder and intestines did not function as they had in his youth. He did not mean to linger there, but he was delayed at the baths by a trickle of water from the fresh water tap. A lengthy line, but Mila did not mind waiting to fill his canteen. A full, wet canteen brought about a small rise in spirits, and for Mila that was reason enough to queue.

The baths were quiet, except for a drunken old reprobate who staggered and sang. Mila had seen the man before, somewhere. The Chinese guards ignored him with their characteristic abhorrence of the insane. The man was free to wander, breaking the peace. Right now he was drunkenly warbling a pop song Mila had heard in the tents: "Everybody Makes Mistakes, Why Can't You Forgive Mine?" His tremulous old voice sounded like a wood rasp:

> *Everybody makes mistakes,*
> *Why can't you forgive mine?*
> *The world is a sorry place,*
> *Forgiveness would be divine.*

It was a pathetic song even for an old drunk to sing, and Mila gave him a pitying glance but had not even a copper to give for barley beer. The drunk returned Mila's look, and for a moment Mila had the strange feeling the man was neither inebriated nor deranged. But when he looked up from the tap, the old fellow had drifted away.

The sun was up and it was noticeably warmer in his tent when he returned with an empty bladder and a full canteen. He set about boiling water to make tea and rice.

Mila's tea was cooling when the first Chinese patrol of the day rumbled past the tents. Mila peered through the flaps. Three open-sided troop carriers went by, cruising slowly, stirring up the dust. Each truck was filled with soldiers, their helmets camouflaged in tan and green. Mila wanted to see their faces, but it was unwise to be observed by a Chinese patrol—he stayed where he was until the trucks had roared out of sight.

By then his tea was tepid, and the rice in its cooker was peppered with dust. Mila tossed the tea into the corner and satisfied his thirst with water from the canteen. He was hungry now, but it was hot in the tent. He retrieved his rice bowl from beneath the brown shawl that covered his few belongings and filled it with rice. Then he went outside to eat his breakfast.

Mila ate his rice hungrily with his handmade *kuaizi*, clicking them against the side of the gray wooden bowl. He had carved the bowl himself from a strange piece of wood brought into the mountains by an old crone smelling of muscatel and coriander who had been to visit relatives in Mumbai, a city by the sea. The wizened old Lha-kha said the wood had drifted up onto the beach from out of the sea, and she had plucked it up from the sand herself to carry back home to Tibet. She called it driftwood. Her family wanted to believe her, but some doubted her story. Mila himself reasoned that no trees grew in the sea—it was like asserting a lake-born lotus on dry, parched land. Mila, who possessed an analytical turn of mind even as a child, was certain that the wood had grown on land and had merely fallen into the sea to drift, but he was too respectful to debate the old woman. Nevertheless, although it was gray, it was most definitely wood, and Mila was very fond of it.

The camp was coming to life. Mila finished his meal and placed chopsticks and bowl beneath his workbench. As he set out his crutch-making tools, he greeted his neighbors on their way to the markets and the baths. Some returned his friendly greeting, but many more reproached him with stone-faced silence. They could not blame the Dalai Lama for their current situation—she was Chenrezig on earth—but Mila had been her minister, her advisor, and (many believed) her fancy man. He was a convenient repository for the waste products of their despair.

He began work on a small crutch for a child named Dorje. A land mine had claimed one of Dorje's legs, and another took the life of Dorje's mother, who never reached her injured son. After the boy had been in the hospital for a while, his father gave Dorje's torn and bloodied trousers to Mila. The child's garment was painful to behold, but it was a fair measurement for the length of the crutch. At first the father had been promised a high-tech prosthesis for his motherless boy; then a low-tech prosthesis; then an aluminum crutch. But like so many promises to the people of New Tibet City, they all vanished into air. Dorje was returning soon from the hospital, and Mila wanted the boy's first wooden crutch to be a good one.

Mila was shaping the arm piece when a shadow fell over his work. He glanced up. Standing before his bench were three thin men and a short, squat women. Mila had met them before. They were a delegation from the Tibetan People's Conciliation Committee. He looked into their unsmiling faces and realized he had been half-expecting their visit. He put down his adze, but said nothing.

The woman, whose name was Pema, snatched the blood-stiff trousers from the workbench and shook them angrily in Mila's face.

"Always more death. Always more destruction. You are to be blamed for this. It is you who are responsible!"

She drew back her arm and threw the pants violently into Mila's face. For a moment Mila was enfolded in the cloying touch of the shredded rags. An image of a young mother crossing a minefield sprang unbidden to his mind. He gagged on an upsurge of bile as the pants fell to the dusty ground.

Mila looked down at the pants, obscurely embarrassed, while the woman went on, her face distorted with anger:

"Have you no shame? Have you no feelings?" She picked up the wooden peg leg of the crutch and waved it at Mila. "That you, of all people, should profit from the suffering of others. You monster! I spit on you!"

Mila looked up and met her eyes. He gazed for a moment into the depths of her fury. Why was he reminded of an eagle? Oh, yes. Tara had told him once of a Greek bodhisattva who fed his liver each day to a hungry bird. He reminded himself that Pema had lost loved ones: a husband, two children. Who here had not?

Tashi, the tallest of the thin men, spoke:

"Mila, we have come to have a word with you on this particular day. Do you know why we have come?"

Mila knew. But he said nothing.

"Of course he knows," sneered Tupten, the next tallest man. "How could he forget? He is a great culpable fool, but not an ass."

"We want you to give us your word," said the third man sternly. "We want your word, Mila—do you hear me?" His name was Dondup.

Mila looked from face to face. There was no escaping their merciless glare. The fierce anger of Pema, in particular, seemed to distort the space around her with its intensity, like the beating of a pair of great wings.

Mila shrugged uneasily. "What can I tell you?"

"Look, he shrugs," cried Pema. "That is his response to all our troubles—an unfeeling shrug. I tell you, he is a heartless monster. We would all be better off without him."

"You can tell us that you will do nothing to anger the Chinese. No public demonstration of support—that is what you can tell us!" yelled Tashi, suddenly losing his composure. "We ask you to promise us that!"

Mila hung his head sadly, but said nothing.

"See? Just as I told you. You can read it in his face. He will make trouble for us again and again, until we are all dead. What kind of a monster is he?"

"Now Pema . . . " began Dondup.

"Pema is right," cried Tupten. "Damn you, Mila! You are killing our children one by one. Will you finally be satisfied when all Tibetans everywhere are dead?"

"It is the Communists who are murdering Tibetans, not I," insisted Mila, raising his head and returning the stares of his accusers.

"What did I tell you?" cried Pema. "You see? You see? He will not mend his ways, he will not promise us anything. He will go on with his mad schemes until we are all dead!" And saying this, she swung the crutch peg she held with all her strength, smashing it down onto the workbench. Mila barely had time to jump back as the stick whistled past his nose.

The tallest man grabbed Pema. "No, no," he cried. "This is forbidden."

"I don't care. I want to kill him!"

Mila looked down in horror at the damage she had wrought. "She has smashed my workbench!" he cried angrily. "And look: she has broken my rice bowl." Mila picked up the two pieces of gray wood and regarded his tormentors with anger in his eyes. "What is the point of this? Please get her out of here. Are you all taken by demons?"

"Not until we get your promise. We demand this, Mila. We want no funny business."

"That's right. They tolerate no public demonstration. The least show of support and they shut off the water for a week."

"I heard five days," corrected Mila stubbornly.

"All right, it is five days. How many died in those five days, the last time some damn fool demonstrated?" demanded Tupten.

"How many died, Mila? Did you ever hear?" cried Dondup.

Mila had heard. Many had died. But he was angry now, and trembling. He threw the driftwood violently onto the ground. The broken pieces of his workbench lay in ruins about his legs. Broken workbench, broken bowl, broken dreams, broken bones, broken vows. . . . Could one man bear all this? It was too much. It was suddenly just too much.

"I want you to go now," said Mila loudly. "Go, before I lose my self-control. But before you go, I will tell you one true thing. If we do not stop the Chinese, they will not rest until we are all dead."

"Stop them?" Dondup laughed bitterly. "There are ten thousand of them to every one of us. How can we stop them? Are you the greatest fanatic in history?"

They were all silent. Mila slowly unclenched his fists. He looked around. A small crowd had gathered. Mila stooped to the rubble of his workbench. It seemed as if he was studying the damage they had done. He picked up the two pieces of the broken crutch, tangled in Dorje's shredded, bloodied pant leg. He paused for a long moment.

"And what about *her*?" he finally asked. "Are we to forget her? Do we just turn our eyes to the south and ignore the fact that she is still there in Narkang Prison? Can you forget her? Can you do that?"

The three men and the woman exchanged glances. Pema muttered something under her breath and spat.

"We are not forgetting her, Mila," said Tashi, the tall one. "You need not worry about that. But you must honor her memory in less prohibited ways. Do you understand?"

"And if I do not?"

"Then we will stop you," said the shortest. And on that threatening note, they turned and marched away.

Mila cleaned up his broken workbench under the thoughtful eyes of his neighbors. Picking up the broken bowl, he experienced a moment of total despair. It was all so hopeless. What could one man do? Mila shook his head sadly. One man could barely make a crutch to hold the weight of a one-legged child. He went back to work on another length of wood.

Later that day, Mila cleaned his tent, threw a few things into a pack, and made his way through a maze of alleys to the merchant quarter. There he came to a chain-link fence surrounding the hill and the charred ruin that had been the Podrang Palace. Razor wire topped the fence, but every child in New Tibet City knew it was possible to slip under the links.

Inside, Mila stood and brushed the dust from his clothes. He looked around cautiously. As usual, there were no guards inside the sacred precinct.

Climbing the ruin was itself dangerous. The broken masonry continued to settle, even after fifteen years. Many pilgrims had hobbled home with twisted ankles and bruised ribs. Although the shifting rubble was treacherous, Mila had recently discovered a good way to the top. He began to climb.

He climbed carefully, stepping slowly from stone to stone. His footsteps stirred clouds of dust, powdering his clothes and skin. The smashed palace still smelled like fire, but the fires were long out, and the ghosts of the dead had drifted away on the smoke. Mila paused again to blow the dust from his nose and memories of war from his mind. Settling his pack, he resumed his climb.

At the top of the pile, Mila shaded his eyes and glanced up at the sun, standing at its zenith in a cloudless blue heaven. Lighting a bundle of *bo* sticks, he prayed while the smoke flowed out over the broad valley. Then, like a man releasing doves, he tossed paper prayer slips to the four quarters. Light winds carried them into the east, a good direction for raising spirits and bringing luck.

Proprieties observed, Mila set down his pack and removed two jointed metal tent poles and a rolled up banner.

He assembled the aluminum tent poles. He screwed one into the rubble and wedged the other between two rocks three meters away. He unrolled the banner. It was rough canvas, with canvas straps sewn onto the ends. Mila used the straps to tie the banner to the poles. It took a long time. His fingers were confused. They trembled. His mind flashed obsessively to memories of his beloved Dalai Lama, of Gunru and Sukyi, of the dog Gochen, and of the boy Dorje.

Finally the banner was in place. A light breeze gently rippled the canvas, on which Mila had painted words in large red letters. The banner was torn from the groundskirts of his tent. A soul in chains, peering through a narrow slit in Narkang Prison, might just be able to make out the red letters:

She Still Lives.

The next day the Army turned off the water.

For two days life continued as usual in the teeming camp. Many families had extra canteens hidden in the coolest recesses of their homes. People rationed their water carefully. No one washed; no one went in the sun without reason.

On the third day the young mine victim, Dorje, came home from the hospital. His father carried him to Mila's tent. The child's horror and pain were etched in lines on his young face; the father's grief was immeasurable; but Mila noted with satisfaction that at least there was no infection in the re-sectioned leg.

The crutch peg was a little too long. Mila altered its length with a plane. The boy took it under his arm with trepidation. Mila showed him how to get around the little space in the tent. Soon he was hopping about splendidly. His stricken face lightened; his father hugged him tearfully.

Mila was pleased. "Dorje is growing. Every few months he will need a longer peg. Bring him back regularly; I will see to it."

"We will do that," said the father. "You have our thanks. How much do I owe you?"

"Nothing. Nothing at all," said Mila.

"What, nothing? How can you live without charging for your work?"

Mila laughed. The same question had crossed his mind.

Dorje spoke for the first time. "Uncle, my papa knows all about you," he said proudly. "I heard him talking."

"He does?" said the surprised Mila, looking at the boy's Dad.

"Dorje, don't tell tales."

"He calls you *changchup semba*. What does that mean, Uncle?"

Mila felt his face grow hot. "In my case, it does not mean anything."

The father looked solemnly at his boy for a moment. He turned to face the maker of his son's crutch.

"Mila," he said, "I hope you do not mind my speaking frankly. I know who you are. You helped lead the demonstrations against the Chinese in the Year of the Tiger. You do not remember me, but I was on the march to the Tsur River and also the Freedom March. We believed in nonviolence. Like you, we thought the Chinese would relent."

Mila regarded the man warmly. "Sure, you are one of the brave ones. But I have been asked to consider that our struggle has only made things worse."

"Certainly, life has become more difficult." The man shrugged with resignation. "This is the degenerate time. But adversity serves to make us stronger." He glanced at his son.

"I am so sorry for your troubles," offered Mila, looking with sympathy from father to son. "But here I am forgetting my manners. Let me offer you both some water."

They drank the warm liquid gratefully. Mila casually pushed his now empty canteen into the shadows as if it still held water. The boy's father continued his anguished speech:

"Everyone on earth has troubles. Here we have known nothing but trouble since our fathers' fathers' time. Things tend downward. When you and I were boys, Mila, the snows fell in August. Now even the Podrang, the city . . . what have we left? Only the minefields it seems are ours forever." Shaking his head, he reached out a strong arm for his son. Father and son comforted each other tenderly. "And now our water is stopped again. Like last year. So what is that? Perhaps some will die of thirst; maybe some will go to the minefields for water. But really, anyone with half a brain has a good supply hidden away. We may be damned, but we cannot stop opposing the Chinese."

Mila nodded his head sorrowfully. "I cannot stop myself from opposing Communist rule, that much is certain. Perhaps the Committee is right. Maybe I am a dangerous fanatic."

"It is the Communists who are dangerous."

Mila spread his hands hopelessly. "I knew they would stop the water. I am the only one to blame."

"She always warned us that it would be difficult," the boy's father reminded Mila gently. "But as she always pointed out, non-cooperation with evil is a sacred duty."

"That was Gandhi," said Mila automatically.

"Really? I thought I heard her say it."

"It has been long since we heard her speak, friend."

After Dorje and his father left his tent, Mila sat for a moment, suddenly weak with hunger. His skin was cold and he felt light-headed. His thoughts spun. He thought of her in the darkness and privation of her prison cell. In his mind, he meditated upon the human Dalai Lama, transforming her into the goddess Tara, protector of the Tibetan people. She glowed green, with graceful arms, endlessly performing enlightened activities for the benefit of all. She is the most beautiful soul in the world, he thought. Adversity has no effect on her. She embraces her captors in an ocean of love.

After his meditation he felt better. He was embraced in an ocean of love, but he had no water. He slept fitfully. In his dreams he heard a confused babble. He awoke with a terrible dryness in his mouth and an aching head. The tent seemed stiflingly hot, but he was not sweating. He lay quietly, in a confused state between sleeping and waking. He heard voices, numerous voices.

Suddenly Mila was wide-awake. After his years in prison, his sense of impending danger was very keen. Kicking free of his bedclothes, he grabbed his empty canteen and slipped ignominiously under the canvas just as an angry crowd came through the front flap.

Dawn of the fourth day found Mila hiding in an ancient drainage pipe on the outskirts of town. The old drains in which Mila lay dated from before his birth. They had been constructed during the early reign of the Sixteenth by a visiting European engineer; choked with weeds and dry from years of drought, they were known of by few.

Where Mila lay was quite near an arm of the Tactical Area. It was a quiet place, and dangerous. No lynching party would come searching for him. Besides, this was the fourth day. Water was too scarce for physical exertion. Canteens were empty. The citizens were sheltering in their tents. Mila knew that early risers were thirstily collecting drops of dew from the canvas. Their faces were glum, hopeless; this would be a day when people drank their own urine. Some would go mad and others would die. The fourth day was a good day for hiding in a drainage pipe.

As the sun rose into the merciless sky, Mila considered his

situation. He could not return home while the water was off; the angry mob would be waiting for him. But if he remained in the sewer, it would not be long before he died of thirst. What options did he have?

Mila looked out across the neighboring field. It appeared harmless enough. Mila could take his chances with the mines, try to cross one of the narrower killing grounds and make his way into the forbidden hills. He wished he had the dog along with him.

Mila had also heard it said that bears patrolled the borders of Tactical Area One, waiting to be allowed to re-enter their ancestral berrying grounds. So angry bears awaited those few who tried to skirt the minefields. The angry bear population on the lower slopes of the Himalayas was on the rise. Once, in the prison court-yard—where over the years so many prisoners had shown Mila their wounds—he had seen the horrible traces of the attack of a bear. The man had lost an arm to the vicious beast, and part of a foot. It was as if a land mine had come into his camp while he was sleeping to explode upon him.

The bear and the land mine, thought Mila. It was bad to encounter either beast in nature, but bears at least did not hide under the earth by the thousands and millions.

It was said that battle-hardened soldiers of the People's Liberation Army, unafraid of death by bullets, missiles, mortars, or nuclear weapons, would kill their commanding officers rather than risk their legs and testicles crossing an unmapped minefield. Mila believed it. Mila understood their fear. He dreaded the Tactical Area more than torture. His insides churned at the thought of tripping a mine. One thing was for certain: he would not be crossing this harmless-looking field today.

So this is where I end up, he thought to himself. In a drain-pipe. It was amusing, really. Well, not really. He was stuck, dying of thirst, between two deadly alternatives. Wasn't it more honorable to die of thirst in the sewer than to allow his fellow humans to murder him? Certainly it was; and Mila took some comfort from that thought, but by mid-morning, Mila was becoming bored with the process of dying of thirst. He hoped it would not last much longer. His lips were cracked and swollen; the tip of his tongue was black. His breathing came in a painful rasp; to swallow was burning pain. Sand seemed to have replaced saliva in his mouth. His sinuses were swelling shut. He felt as if he had been struck on the nose with a club (and he knew that feeling well). His eyes were unfocused and irritated by dry granules. Most painfully, his mind ran on, out of control. As the sun rose higher in the sky, heating his cramped space unmercifully, Mila's thoughts turned against him. For a while, as he drifted in and out of consciousness, he was convinced that the ticking of the metal pipe as it expanded was the sound of cool rain falling on forested hills. He saw himself immersed to the neck in a cool mountain lake; he could feel his body heat dispersing in the water, and he shivered deliciously with cold. But strangely, when he lowered his head to drink a delightful draught of water, the liquid fled from his lips, which remained cracked and dry, and his tongue swelled to fill the inside of his rough-skinned mouth.

Sometimes he opened his eyes to find a world of darkness and sparks, though he knew it should be daylight; sometimes he could see the sun. But each awakening was a painful return to his thirst. Around noon he decided to drink his own urine, but his bladder was empty. Mila lost his grip soon after. He decided the Chinese had somehow turned off his urine along with the water. He began drafting in his mind a letter of protest to some imaginary Tibetan newspaper in defense of his right to urinate. He spoke the words out loud, raving.

His moments of clarity dissolved in swirls of delirium. He drifted amidst his memories of Narkang Prison. He lay on the straw matting and heard vividly the rattle-clang of his cell's iron door. Nothing was required of the prisoner at this point. Everything depended on what happened next. If the guard took two steps across the stone floor and kicked him in the ribs with a steel-toed boot, all was well. He would arise and go to the exercise yard. But if the man turned and locked the cell door behind him, that was bad news. He lay silently, hoping for the kick.

He came around for an hour of consciousness. He tried his best to pray. But late in the afternoon, with the sun directly in his face, Mila lost contact with reality again. In his vision he was standing in a baseball stadium somewhere in China. It was beastly hot. He was on the infield with dozens of other Tibetan prisoners. The stands were filled with cheering spectators. A black-clad torturer explained the rules of the very simple game. A prisoner donned the black hood—just the one hood for everyone—then sprinted full speed to smash into the outfield wall. The fastest runner could retire from the game. The slowest would be fed to the bears—there were bears along the foul line. The game would be played on and on and on. The game would never stop being played.

Mila was filled with horror at the fiendish game that had been devised for them. It was inhuman sport. A prisoner could refuse to participate in their pitiless fun, and be torn apart by bears. Alas, that fate seemed unavoidable, since Mila's legs were very weak, and he doubted they would carry him into the wall. He heard a meaty thud. The crowd cheered wildly. Mila was next up. His head was covered by the bag. Mila smelled the clotted blood and the odor of fear. He began to faint, felt his knees buckle. Suddenly, a strange thing happened: he was no longer the man in the stifling hood; he was a bear watching a pitiable human in a black hood collapse to the ground. It took a moment for Mila to orient himself to his new sense perceptions. His vision was far poorer than usual, but his sense of smell was greatly amplified. It was almost as it had been with Gochen, the sniffer dog. He could smell the other bears. He could smell the crowd as a whole and individually. He could smell the sweat-soaked leather of the prisoner's hood—the disgusting reek of human fear, the infuriating scent of blood. Mila had somehow projected his consciousness into the bear. He had heard of such powers, a supernatural power of the adept. It was said that magicians in the hills casually entered into the bodies of foxes, geese, bears. The new hosts were most often recently deceased. Mila looked down at his ferocious claws. The thick muscles of the bear's neck were not as flexible as his human musculature but, looking up, he observed a bird soaring high above the stadium. Mila felt trapped and hot inside the thick coat of fur. The bird looked cool and free. He decided to project his mind into the bird and, just as suddenly, he found himself high in the air, dipping and wheeling over the stadium, feeling the rush of wind as keen exhilaration under his primary feathers. His eyes were sharp. He kept his old body in view. He felt a surprising attachment to the collapsed human. What would happen to him now? How could he return to his old body? Perhaps he could not return. It would be too bad: human bodies are rare. But being a bird is good too, dreamed Mila. Simply by sailing on the wind, I can teach everyone in Tibet to fly to freedom.

He sailed across the valley on an updraft toward a ridge of low hills. Wondering now what kind of bird he had become, Mila dove low over a mountain lake to observe his reflection. Suddenly overcome by thirst, he spilled wind from his wings to plunge into the water of the lake. But there was no water. Instead, the ground exploded upwards and smashed into his head.

Mila came around slowly, feeling the pain in his nose as if from a distance. He greedily licked the blood that flowed from it. He was back in his hellishly hot pipe. What a terrible disappointment! He hadn't flown in the body of the bird at all. He had not been in the bear. Mila became afraid for his disintegrating mental state. It was time to get out of the drainage pipe. He might as well die in the open; it would be a death less cruel. However, when he tried to move, he found his legs would not function. He had become too weak to move either forward or back. He struggled for a while then gave up, exhausted.

The next time Mila regained consciousness, it was dark. Someone was singing nearby. Mila stuck his blackened tongue out of his crusted mouth and waggled it in the cool night air. He was pretty sure he was about to die, although he could not help noticing that the voice he heard singing was not that of an angel. In fact, it sounded like an old drunk warbling the popular tune "Everybody Makes Mistakes, Why Can't You Forgive Mine?"

The off-key singing stopped. Mila saw a scuffed and mended sandal just inches from his nose. He tried to touch it with a claw-like hand, but the effort was too great. He blacked out.

The next Mila knew, he was standing propped against a tree. Something had improved—water flowing into his mouth. He swallowed gratefully. The old fellow sitting beside him was administering water from a full, wet canteen. Mila felt his spirits lift.

"More water," he choked out happily—his entire universe in two words.

"Well, well," said the disreputable old fellow. "Here's a thirsty soul. You need more than water, old daddy." He tipped the canteen up for Mila to drink. "How did you get stuck in that drain? Too much *chang*?"

"Hiding," sputtered Mila. He took the canteen from the man's hand and put it up to his mouth, draining a blessed pint.

"Sorry," he gasped, ashamed of his need.

"Help yourself," said the other kindly. He was tall and fatherly, with a toothless old head atop the body of an old athlete. "I got three canteens. And there's plenty of water where I'm going."

"Thank you." Mila poured more liquid down his throat. His entire body seemed to awaken, like a dried-out sponge.

"Hiding, eh?" the old man asked slyly. "From the fucking Army?"

"The Committee," Mila gasped between mouthfuls of water.

"Ah. Damned committees. They get a man down." He peered more carefully at his companion. "You are Mila Lakpa. I did not recognize you under all that grime. Do you remember me from the lists?"

"You are Jamyang Tashi, sure. Congratulations on your release, old friend."

"Gunru told me he would see you."

"Gunru and his sister are arrested. The dog is dead."

"Oh? Crap. That is bad luck."

"What are you doing in New Tibet City? Gunru said you were the mayor of some mountain village but here I see you at the latrines. You regaled us with your . . . singing."

"Not a big fan, eh? Everyone is a music critic, even people you pull out of drains."

Mila smiled weakly. "Your singing is of the very worst. But I thank you for pulling me from the drain."

Jamyang laughed. "Okay, you are a truthful man, Mila, so I will give it to you straight in return. There is a Chinese patrol on the next hill over. Can you hear them? If they find you, they will assuredly shoot you for violating curfew. Maybe me too, although they think I am insane."

As he spoke, Mila could hear the dogs baying over the ridge.

"Then you have wasted good water on a dead man, my friend," Mila told his rescuer apologetically, returning the canteen to him. "For I cannot return to my tent while the water is off. The Committee is after my head."

"Yes, and who can blame them? Look what trouble you have caused, with your silly demonstration."

"My sincere regrets hardly matter now. As you point out, I will soon be dead."

"You will most certainly be shot if you stay here. But I suggest you come with me."

"With you? And where might you be going?"

"Didn't Gunru tell you? I am the proud Mayor of Freetown, the revolutionary capitol of Tactical Area One." He beamed with pride.

"*Kun cho sum!*" breathed Mila, eyes gone wide. "You are as mad as poor Gunru."

"Oh, we are not so bad," laughed Jamyang. "Just a little different from you and our beloved **Kundun.**"

"Different?" said Mila suspiciously. "In what way?"

A sudden gust of wind brought the barking of dogs. Mayor Jamyang corked his canteen and stood up quickly.

"We can talk at length when we reach the safety of the hills," he said. "Will you come and live with the brave citizens of Freetown, or will you stay and feed the dogs?"

Mila looked over his shoulder uneasily. "Your argument has merit," he conceded. "Why give them the satisfaction? I have never been a great fancier of Army dogs."

"Just so," said Jamyang, shouldering his tawdry bundle. "Although they are damned good if stewed with onions and potatoes."

4

Mayor Jamyang led Mila north and then east around the perimeter of New Tibet City, leaving the baying of the dogs well behind. Soon they came to the border of Tactical Area One. This steep terrain had long been abandoned by Tibetans and Chinese alike. Wild grasses blew in the night breeze while heavy timber stood guard over the dangerous ground. The barking of the guard dogs was very faint now, and the crescent moon was partially obscured behind ragged clouds. Mila, in his weakened state, could not keep from stumbling over the uneven ground, barely able to match the pace of Jamyang, who had found his stride unerringly in the dark.

"Make sure you stay right behind me," he called over his shoulder to Mila. "Step only where I have stepped. There are many mines in these hills."

Many mines. Mila's fear increased with every eastward step. There had been no fence or warning sign to indicate their passage into the killing ground—only an oppressive silence. At first they passed craters on the left and right, and in some of them there were scattered bones, dimly glowing in the moonlight. Nothing stirred. Owls flew overhead. No creatures larger than a Tibetan shrew ventured into this area. Vultures feasted on the remains of those who did. There were ghosts, and Mila could feel their presence, but he could not see them. The pair gained altitude. Jamyang continued his upward progress confidently, and Mila struggled to stay close behind him.

Step after step the miles went by, Mayor Jamyang moving confidently forward, and the flash and bang that Mila expected did not come. He began to believe they were on a safe path to Freetown.

"I wish we had that dog," muttered Jamyang at one point.

The moon came out from behind the clouds, revealing upturned ground. Stars wheeled overhead and clouds came and went. Sometimes Mila walked with a clear head, sometimes in a daze. Sometimes his legs cramped and he had to stop. Then he would carefully hurry to catch up with the Mayor. Every hour or so Jamyang would stop, uncork the canteen, and he and Mila would drink. They spoke little. Toward morning they turned north again. Lightning outlined a mountain ridge just ahead of them. But the moon had gone down, and Mayor Jamyang seemed less certain of the trail. He paused from time to time, sniffing the air like a bloodhound.

"Are we through the mines?" Mila asked hopefully.

"Not yet. But very soon."

"You are still sure of the way, are you not?"

Jamyang chuckled. "It would be easier in the daylight. But we cannot risk much travel in the day."

"I take it the Army has never found your camp?"

"Affirmative. Freetown is in an isolated ravine. There are numerous caves. The Army cannot see us with their satellites or helicopters. They may know we are in the region, but if they come, we are ready for them."

"You would oppose them with violence?" asked Mila.

Mayor Jamyang laughed. "Would that be so terrible? We Tibetans have been nonviolent for hundreds of years, and look at us."

"We cannot beat the Chinese with violence."

"Come Mila, don't be so naive. Satyagraha worked against the British. It worked in the American South. But it will never work against the Chinese."

"The world has not yet seen the full power of satyagraha," maintained Mila.

"Well, it is hard to know who is right. Look, I have found the path again. I thought we had wandered into the mines. For a second there, we were dead men. Ha ha! It is this way."

The man could make light of their extreme peril, but when the Mayor began walking again, Mila concentrated on placing his feet exactly in the steps of the other man. They began to climb a steep hill in the dark. Soon they were grasping bushes and clumps of grass, pulling themselves up the worst spots. Eventually they reached a bare granite ridge.

"We can relax now," said the Mayor. "The mines are mostly behind us, now."

"Can we rest?"

"No. We must move even more quickly. Soon it will be light. We have a few kilometers to go. Can you can make it?"

"As long as there is water, there is hope," ventured Mila. It was the sort of thing he felt a brave man might say.

He and Jamyang climbed side by side up the high ridge. In olden days the mountains would have been covered with a thick blanket of snow at this altitude. Higher up, the glacial ice would have reflected the stars. But now there was ice no more, and it had been years since it had snowed.

The absence of mines lifted their spirits and made their march more companionable. As dawn lit the granite peaks with a violet hue, Mila and Jamyang were crossing a high mountain pass.

"Perfect timing," said the Mayor. "Mila, I admire your stamina. Now we descend into Freetown. Please watch your footing. The going is very steep."

The descent was dangerous, and Mila was feeling the depths of his tiredness, yet he remained sure-footed. As daylight streamed over the mountains, they entered a narrow ravine. Mayor Jamyang announced their entrance into Freetown. A boulder-strewn stream ran through the center of the divide. Mila threw himself down beside it and drank thirstily from his cupped hands, and when he had enough, he splashed water over his face and neck until his skin tingled with cold. Mayor Jamyang knelt beside him and did the same.

The two men kneeled in the cold mountain water and grinned at each other like a pair of fools.

"I am always like this when I come from the city," admitted Jamyang. "That place is so damned dry. Even without your meddling."

"I hope they have turned the water on by now."

"Oh, they have. Didn't I tell you? They turned it back on the night we left."

"I am very grateful to hear it."

Mila looked around. To the west rose a magnificent range of mountain peaks. To the east rose another range, even higher. Mila realized they had come into this valley over one of those ranges, but he was too tired and disoriented to determine which.

"Tell me, Mayor, where are the others?"

"It is early morning. There are thirty of us now, mostly in the hills, keeping guard or hunting game."

They heard a distant voice hailing the Mayor. Looking up, they saw a man on the hill waving a hunting rifle.

"It is Basang Uri Garma," said Jamyang happily. "You remember him, do you Mila? We marched together for a number of years. Basang is a sharpshooter and a good demolitions man."

"I did not know that."

"Back in the old days, Basang fought without weapons. He is as brave as a lion."

Basang came scrambling down the hill into the ravine. He was a short, stocky man with unbound hair and a white-toothed smile. He wore buckskin breeches and crossed belts of ammo over a green brocade jacket. He had a muscular torso. His ancient rifle was augmented with an antique optical sniper scope. It glistened with sweet oil.

"Is this our Mila, back from the dead?" he cried.

"Uri Garma, a pleasure to see you again. Congratulations on your release."

"Aye, and yours, Mila." he said, grasping Mila's hand.

"He *was* responsible for the water shut off," Jamyang confirmed to his friend.

"What a fellow!" grinned Basang. "Brave but dumb—that about describe it, Mila?"

"I am afraid dumb alone describes it," said Mila. The Tibetan word they were using for "dumb" was descriptive of hopeless imbeciles. "I was terrified they would catch me."

Basang laughed delightedly. "Well, you are in good company here. None of us has even a glimmer of intelligence. If we did, we'd be over the mountains into India."

"Tibet has the better climate."

"How do you come to be here in Freetown, Basang?"

"I was in the camps with Jamyang. We were released at the same time."

"We saw a floater earlier today," Jamyang suddenly remembered, referring to a Chinese helicopter he and Mila had spotted after dawn. "About two clicks north. It looked to be flying a recon pattern."

"They are starting to bring them back from Xinjiang. One of these days we may have to re-evaluate our position. Mila, want to come with us on a short patrol?"

"I need sleep," Mila admitted.

"Here is my cave," said Mayor Jamyang, pulling aside a

screen of brush and vines, revealing a shallow indentation in the rock. The men entered.

Mila observed the bedding, an untidy bundle of rags, with a pang of pleasure.

"Ah," sighed Mila, "all the comforts of home."

"Sleep, Mila, sleep. If we return with game, I will awaken you for a feast."

"I am hoping for another bear this month," grinned Basang. "The last one was very delicious."

"And if there is no game?" asked Mila. "What do we eat?"

Mayor Jamyang spread his hands in an attitude of disinterested acceptance. "There is water. Some sage once said, while there is water, there is hope."

Basang shook his head. "I am not worried. The fruit is lying on the ground and there are sure to be bears."

The men went into the hills and Mila slept.

He awoke a few hours later to the sound of harsh voices barking orders in Chinese. I am in Narkang Prison, he thought with a sinking heart. But he rejected the idea immediately. The air in his mouth was too fresh, and there was bedding under his head. Freetown, he thought with relief. *But there are no Chinese in Freetown!*

The voices were very close. Mila got to his knees and crawled to the screen of branches. He slowly pushed the foliage aside until he could see out of the cave. His heart pounded in his chest—the valley had been discovered by a company of soldiers. He knew their green uniforms, their soft caps with the red star, their modern automatic weapons with laser sights and folding stocks. He could not see any vehicles. The company must have walked in from the north. Six soldiers were herding a group of women into a cave directly opposite.

Mila was very afraid. The sight of PLA uniforms brought back bad memories. Involuntarily, on all fours like an animal, he began backing into the rear of the cave. Strange growling noises came from his throat. He began panting hoarsely. If there had been an exit into a minefield, Mila would have run out into it. So, he thought to himself, at least this answers the question of what you are most afraid of. It is them.

After a while his heart stopped pounding quite so hard against his ribs. The loud voices had ceased. Mila, at the back wall of the cave, could see out through the screen of vines. Only one soldier stood guard over the mouth of the cave where they had placed the women. He carried a large machine pistol. The other soldiers were gone. They have gone to find the men, thought Mila.

His mouth was very dry. Looking around for one of Mayor Jamyang's canteens, Mila saw that he was kneeling in a blackened campfire pit. Sharp stones dug into his knees. At his right hand, leaning against the rock, was an old black iron wok. He moved the wok to one side, revealing an oily rag. Wrapped in the rag was a large chopping knife. It had a thick square blade with a shining sharp edge. It had a wooden handle with some faded red paint remaining at the heel.

Mila looked at the knife for a long, quiet moment. Never before in his life had he contemplated killing anyone. But then, killing had never before been an option. All of his campaigns had been waged with the Dalai Lama, an infuriating but superior being who did not show anger or doubt in her nonviolent dealings with the Chinese.

Nonviolent but disastrous, he thought, suddenly picking up the knife and hefting it in his hand.

It was heavy. He touched his thumb to the blade. It was razor sharp. He looked out of the cave at the soldier, who now had his back to him, shouting something cheerfully obscene to his retreating comrades.

He imagined slamming the heavy blade into the back of the

man's neck, just above the cloth collar, below the hairline. A hot trembling invaded his every limb. He began to perspire.

I could never get to him in time, thought Mila. He would hear me coming through the vines.

So he must come to you, he said to himself.

Mila stood slowly. His knees were weak. Gripping the knife in his right hand, he went to the front of the cave. A large rock to the left of the opening would hide him from view. He raised the knife over his head and, taking a small pebble from the ground, he tossed it at the wok.

Plunk!

Mila moved his head slightly to look out. The soldier had turned. He had heard something, but he did not know what. He slowly raised his weapon and scanned the ravine, the movement of the big machine pistol synchronized with the movement of his eyes. Mila looked at the man more closely. Not a man, really. More of a boy. Just a young fellow, too thin for his uniform. He looked like a rawboned farm youth dressed for a military parade. His eyes were afraid.

As are mine, thought Mila, perspiring heavily. In his entire life he had never killed anything intentionally, not even an insect. A wild feeling of terror and exultation filled his belly.

This young man is going to die, thought Mila. I do not want him dead, but I cannot let him live. I am only the instrument of his terrible karma. And my own.

Mila's arm holding the knife above his head began to shake. He picked up a slightly larger pebble and threw it with more force against the wok.

Clang!

The soldier fired his weapon into the cave. The sound was deafening. For a moment the space in the cave was filled with flying chips of rock and ricocheting fragments of jacketed shells. Then it stopped. A small cloud of smoke wafted into the cave through the destroyed screen of foliage. A small piece of rock had notched Mila's ear. He felt the warm blood on his neck and the sharp sting of the wound.

Mila waited, holding his breath in the deafening silence.

First the muzzle of the weapon appeared in the opening, like the questing head of a serpent. Mila noted its thickened snout and blunt sight. A wisp of smoke arose from its mouth. The gun barrel entered the cave inch by slow inch. It was less than a foot from Mila's chest. He could have reached out and burned his flesh on the hot metal.

At that moment a strange thing happened. In one instant he was Mila, standing in the cave with a trembling arm raised above his head, looking down on the weapon of a PLA corporal. In the next instant he was standing just outside the cave, looking fearfully in, sharing the heart of the frightened soldier.

Mila was looking out of the other man's eyes; he was hearing the other man's thoughts. The soldier's name was Wu Xiao Chien, an enlisted man serving out his third year in the People's Liberation Army. His dissolute friends in the Chengdu discos called him "Jimmy." He was newly stationed in the rugged mountains of Xizang province, and he did not like it, but he had been transferred from the Chengdu Military Region as a punishment for drunkenness. Oh, how he regretted being caught drunk in the streets of Nanjing by the Military Police! But his regret had not translated into reform. He still liked his *jiu*. He was, after all, a soldier.

Jimmy had heard something; the sound came from this cave. It sounded to him like a weapon being cocked, though it might have been a rock vole. He had unloaded several rounds without investigating further, but now that he was looking at it, the cave had been suspiciously hidden behind a screen of vines. Someone Tibetan was in there, he was sure of it. Damned Tibetans were everywhere in these hills, setting ambushes, springing their devilish traps. He had killed whoever was in the cave, of course, firing in a z-pattern as he had been taught in basic training. Nothing in that cave was alive, and he would just take a very cautious look in there to confirm it now. He wished Sergeant Sun were here. The Sergeant was a veteran of the Peninsular campaign. But Jimmy had handled this well on his own and might even get a commendation. The more commendations he received, the more certain he would be to see the superb discos of Nanjing again. Remember Doris? Remember Lulu? But what if the sound had come from a child? They had not yet found any children in these hills. Please ancestors do not let it be a child. He could never forget killing a child, and to make things worse, it would no doubt be a child of one of those unfortunate women behind him in the first cave. So now he would take a quick, cautious look to confirm that he had not killed a child. He moved forward another foot . . .

With an abrupt dislocation, Mila left the head of Corporal Wu, where he had been staring out of the man's eyes and having the man's thoughts as if they were his own eyes and thoughts. He was back in his own body, feeling disoriented and confused. His eyes did not move, for they had never wavered from the rifle barrel slowly penetrating the cave. The Corporal was coming in now, and there were perhaps two seconds left before his head would appear. Now that he had been in the man's head, Mila knew the Corporal had not suspected that there was a ledge of rock hiding a homicidal Tibetan devil with a butcher knife. He drew in his breath and held it.

Mila watched the Corporal's hand appear, curling tight around the wooden stock of his weapon, just as they had taught him in basic training. Mila felt panic rising in his heart. The soldier's fingers relaxed, shifted their grip, and tightened again on the wooden stock. Mila knew the Corporal was nervous—he could still feel the intensity of it.

At that moment Mila unleashed his blow, and the knife blade came slamming down on the soldier's hand. The man screamed and fell forward into the cave, dropping his weapon and clutching at his severed fingers. He looked up at Mila, who had raised the butcher knife again for the deathblow. But Mila looked into the man's eyes and froze.

"Do you surrender?" Mila demanded of him in Mandarin.

The soldier looked at him with surprise and terror. "I surrender! I surrender! Please do not kill me! My name is Wu. My serial number is . . . "

"Shut up!" Mila thundered. He had to think. So it was true. Somehow he had been inside this soldier's head. He had tasted the man's humanity, heard his prayer to the ancients. Sure, Mila knew they could be friends or even brothers. The blood spurting from Wu's injured hand was not only Chinese blood, it was human blood. Mila could not drive a blade into this man's skull. The butcher knife fell from his hand and took a bounce toward the entrance of the cave. Feeling suddenly very faint, Mila sat down heavily.

"Shit, I can't kill you," he said hopelessly.

Corporal Wu's frightened eyes darted to the entrance of the cave. He screamed at the sight of what he saw there. Mila looked up at the triumphant, not-young face of a Tibetan woman peering in through the entrance. The face was a flat oval, framed with long black hair, with high cheekbones and bright, angry eyes. Three other women were behind her. A slender brown fist reached in quickly and closed around the handle of the butcher knife. There was nothing Mila could do to stop them. The women leaped into the cave roaring like tigers. They were all over the luckless Corporal in seconds, obscuring him from Mila's sight with their flying black hair. But he *could* see the butcher knife rise and fall, rise and fall. Blood splattered everywhere. Wu's screams went on and on. It took him a long time to die. The women grabbed the dead soldier's legs and dragged him outside. His weapon caught in his uniform. It skittered across the rock. Mila crawled away from the steaming puddle of blood and retched onto the stones.

Before Mila had fully recovered, two of the women re-entered the cave, including the slender woman with long dark hair who had done most of the butcher work. They had washed the blood from themselves and donned the *chuba*, as is right in the presence of an unmarried man. Their hair was bound demurely in twisted braids. The women carried sheaves of brush and buckets of water. They went about their work with no more than a few shy glances at the subdued Mila.

What have they done with the Corporal's body? Mila wondered. He decided not to ask about it, and the women did not offer Mila pleasantries. When they had swept and sluiced the bloody stones, they bowed politely and left. Almost immediately the one who had held the knife returned with another bucket of water. For drinking, she said. He thanked her weakly. She placed Jamyang's punctured wok by the mouth of the cave. Returning to Mila's side, she squatted on her haunches, folded her hands in her lap, and waited. Mila realized she was waiting for him to speak. What could he say to her? Please desist from murdering Chinese soldiers with butcher knives, Miss?

"What about Mayor Jamyang and the other men?" he asked, clearing his throat.

"They have gone to kill Chinese." Her voice was soft, with a lovely Central Tibetan accent.

"No doubt they will be pleased with the way you have acted here."

She looked at him quizzically. "But you are not pleased. What would you have had us do with him? He would have killed us all."

Mila sighed. "I have often heard that said."

"You have seen the way they are. Jamyang tells us you are Mila Lakpa."

"I used to be," Mila agreed. "Now I am Mila, maker of crutches. And yes, I have seen the way they are." I have also seen the way we are, thought Mila, but he did not say so. Instead he asked her name.

"I am called Dolma," she told him.

"Wife of Jamyang?"

"No, no. I am the widow of Donyu. He who has been dead now these seven years."

Mila looked at her with more sympathy. Her silence told him everything. Tibetans communicate much without words. Still he asked:

"Are you certain he is dead?" In Tibet, "dead" is a word that sometimes means "imprisoned."

"Oh, yes. I saw him die."

"And the children?" He did not wish to pry, but it was typical for Tibetans to exchange tragic stories. Seven years, he thought. That is probably enough time for her to be able to speak of it.

"Yes. Them too."

"I am so sorry."

"Then I was taken by the soldiers." Dolma looked at him with a quiet, alert expression in her dark eyes. Mila knew the meaning of the silence and the dark look.

"I am so sorry," he said again, placing his palms together and bowing over them. "It must have been very difficult for you."

"Thank you. I lived through the experience, unlike many others. When I was released, I began begging in the tents. You understand?"

Mila understood. After she had been raped, no Tibetan man would marry her. There were many unfortunates such as Dolma in New Tibet City. Sometimes they starved to death in the street if they could not sell their bodies in the alley.

"How did you come to Freetown?" Mila asked Dolma.

"Jamyang found me one night after curfew. I was hiding in the ruins. He came along singing some terrible Chinese song. At first I was too afraid to go off with him. I thought he was a wrathful spirit. But Jamyang was persuasive."

"Especially considering the alternatives."

"Just so. Then he brought me to Freetown. He brought all of us here. At first there were many of us. But many died finding passage through the mines."

Mila remembered the scattered bones in the pale moonlight. Just the bones of some citizens, he thought, working out a path through the mines. Such a small victory over the Chinese, purchased at such a high price.

Just then, they heard distant gunfire. Mila could make out the familiar sound of PLA machine guns, some small-arms fire, and then a series of rippling explosions that surprised Mila, until he thought of the expertise of Basang. Then nothing. They waited out a period of silence. The guns did not fire again.

Mila turned to say something to Dolma, but he held his tongue. Instead he said a small prayer for the Chinese soldiers. The look in her eyes told him they were all dead.

"The men will be coming back soon," Dolma told him. "Perhaps one of them has trapped an animal. I mean an animal a person can eat." Her eyes were shining, but her attitude was perfectly demure. Her slender hands were clasped in her lap. Mila had to remind himself that one of them had wielded the knife. They sat together for a time in companionable silence.

"Speaking of food," said Mila, "I seem to be famished. I have not eaten anything but dried apricots in a very long time."

Dolma looked up with concern. "Of course. How thoughtless I have been. I saw there was no food in your stomach, nothing but green bile. I will bring you some *tsampa* and warm soup. Please wait."

"No, no, I do not need anything to eat." Then he reconsidered. "Well, all right. Thank you. But I will come with you. I have had enough of this cave for now."

Mila and Dolma went out into the daylight. The fresh mountain air cleared the sharp smell of blood from his head. Mila looked around with pleasure. The weather was brisk. Wildflowers covered the slanting hillsides with a carpet of yellow and green. Wu was dead and Lakpa lived.

Dolma led him up the mountain through heavy timber to a campsite at the edge of a high meadow. There was a cook pot suspended on a tripod over a dead fire. Dolma struck a light and directed Mila to collect wood. A cache of spoon-greens and flour was hidden nearby. Soon she was stewing noodles and boiling greens. She spooned barley flour into a battered tin mess kit and softened it with hot tea. She went on with her preparations while Mila rolled large balls of barley dough and devoured them hungrily.

Mayor Jamyang and Basang arrived back in camp, faces blackened with smoke. They carried a load of captured weaponry and heavy belts of ammunition. The men were visibly tired, but they greeted Mila cheerfully enough. More grizzled partisan fighters emerged from the darkness into the firelight and unloaded their gear and booty. They stared curiously at Mila, who nodded at them with a mouth full of *tsampa*. It struck Mila that the partisans all shared the same look: grimly happy to be alive.

Mila swallowed. "Was anyone hurt?"

"We lost one man. Puntsok, brother of Ganden. Just a boy, really. We misjudged the time they would enter the ravine. Puntsok was out of position, and they opened fire on him."

"He was killed?"

"Probably he was killed by their first volley, but certainly he was dead by the time Basang exploded his dynamite because they were standing around his body in a semicircle, firing single shots into it."

Basang shook his head in wonderment. "Could they make it any easier on my conscience?"

The men took their places around the fire. Someone had caught a brace of rabbits, which Dolma skinned and roasted on captured bayonets. Everyone was hungry. Basang had a sack filled with Army rations. He opened a tin of peaches and poured it into his mouth. The thick syrup glistened on his ruddy face. How sweet! He opened another.

Three women entered the cave with a stack of wooden bowls. Jamyang introduced them and they bowed demurely. They had already met, but none of the women seemed eager to mention this. One named Sonam was bold enough to look directly at Mila. Their eyes locked for a brief moment of understanding. The women were not going to mention the incident in the cave. Mila nodded slowly in silent collusion. After all, they had surely saved his life.

While they ate, the men spoke among themselves of the fighting they had done that day, and the women served them silently as if they had not slaughtered an enemy soldier all by themselves. Perhaps they were all used to the bloodshed. They were a wild enough crew. They ate steadily, like hungry beasts, Mila one of them, wolfishly chewing his piece of charred rabbit.

After the meal they sat around the fire. They smoked mountain hemp and exchanged stories. Mila refused the intoxicating smoke, but not the stories. His years in prison had left him abstemious, but hungry for human contact. Mayor Jamyang told him how Freetown had recently been attacked twice by army patrols. They had taken more casualties in the first attack, but in both instances had completely destroyed the enemy.

"With dynamite." Basang grinned horribly around a mouthful of greens.

"Basang saw the floater in the hills to the north," Jamyang continued. "They are looking for us. There can be no doubt about it. Someday they will send a large force into these mountains; perhaps someday soon." But Basang shook his head in disagreement.

"They are too fearful and stupid," he sneered.

"We will see. Anyway, today there was only a small patrol. We went north to greet them, but they must have circled around between us and camp. It was sheer luck they did not find Freetown."

Even now the women did not speak of their blood-soaked afternoon. Mila did not quite understand their reticence, although he was prepared to honor it. Surely it was not that the men would deplore their violence. It must be something else. Mila stared vaguely around him in the dark cave. The cave slanted downward into the dank earth, branching into small alcoves as it went. Plenty of snug places for hiding . . . Jimmy's assault weapon.

"We found a very nice little ravine we knew we could lure them into," the Mayor was saying for the tenth time. "Basang built them a sweet little trap with his dynamite. We got tired of waiting, so we sent the twins south to find the patrol. The twins had just gone beyond the ridge and Puntsok was coming back from taking a crap when the patrol came into the ravine from the north."

Basang held up his hands by way of demonstration. He looked as if he were holding a lotus stem in each hand. He touched his hands together quickly. "Pop," he said simply. "Pop, pop, pop."

"Awful carnage," agreed Mayor Jamyang. "Mila, you are lucky you stayed in camp with the women. I know you hate violence."

Mila looked around at the circle of Freetown men and women. More had arrived, and were sitting easily around the fire enjoying a quiet meal. Mila thought they were a typical Tibetan group, except for two men sitting a little away from the fire who might have been twins. Mila stared in fascination: he had never seen twins before. Twins were virtually unheard of in Tibet, where the Chinese imposed a one-child rule.

Jamyang saw Mila looking at the twins, and he gestured at them. "They are they fastest men in the hills," he bragged. "Purbu jumped down into the ravine and opened fire to keep them in the box; Pemba firing down on them. Oh, yes," Jamyang rubbed his grease-covered hands with glee, "they ran right into our laps. I saw them coming through the timber. They were city fellers, I could tell. When we had them in the box, we opened fire. Did you hear it?"

Mila nodded. "I could hear it, yes."

"They ran up the ravine into a sheltered bowl. It was the tactical thing to do."

"Just what we wanted them to do," smiled Basang with a bloodthirsty glint in his eye. "Pop, pop!" He laughed delightedly. "You see, Mila," he said, displaying his excellent teeth, "you will not find many white robes here in Freetown. We are fighters here."

"You fought in white robes too," said Mila mildly.

"He means we are real fighters, the kind that get results," explained another man dryly, a Freetowner whom Mila had not seen earlier.

"This is Nyima," said Mayor Jamyang, taking a pull on the hemp. Mila nodded at the new man, whose face looked a shade more Han than Tibetan.

"Tell Mila about yourself, Nyima. Tell him how you know so much about getting results, Nyima."

"Shall I tell you my family history?" asked Nyima, looking at Mila for a sign of interest.

"I would enjoy that above everything."

"Although I am half-Chinese and was born in Beijing, I consider myself Tibetan. At the time of the previous Dalai Lama, my mother's ancestors still lived in Tibet. There was a famous lama: Nyar-Tong Rinpoche. Do you remember him? He was a learned lama, certainly not a monk. He was well-known for his desires, like a river, as you can imagine from the fact that he has twenty-seven grandchildren, of whom I am one."

"Surely not the Nyar-Tong who conducted tours of hell?"

"Not only did he conduct tours of hell, but he was also able to find specific souls in torment, could lead a person right up to his old bastard of a father, say. For a very reasonable price. He used mantra and a magic carpet inlaid with a mandala of the eighteen hells. I never had the pleasure, but they say he lived a very humble life, giving much of his money to the women who bore his children."

"What happened to him?"

"Just when his fame as a tour guide of the hells was growing large, there was a bloody government purge—nothing unusual for those vicious times—and the new Party leader, a hardliner named Shu Eng Lei, had his political opponent hanged by the neck on a Japanese cable show called **Public Execution!** Shu Eng Lei appeared on the show as a guest. He read a statement denouncing his opponent for treason and promising to engage the services of a famous magician in order to gloat over his sufferings in hell."

"He had no doubt that his enemy was going to hell?" said Mila.

"He had no doubt. So after the hanging Shu Eng Lei had my grandfather brought to Beijing on a military airplane, along with his magic carpet, and his bells, and all that other lama bullshit."

"Be careful what you say about your grandfather," said the superstitious Jamyang.

"Oh, I think my grandfather had the power, all right. And he had balls. He told Shu Eng Lei that hell was not for gloating. But Shu Eng Lei pretended not to hear him."

"Then what happened?"

"A private ceremony was arranged in a government suite at the Beijing Hilton. Only the principals and a few bodyguards and aides were in attendance. The Hilton supplied a delicious *dim sum*, I have been told. My grandfather prayed over Shu Eng Lei and then sat in silent meditation. Then they lay down on their backs with their heads touching in the center of the carpet. More mantra. They slid into a deep trance.

"The bodyguards and aides sat in silence while the minutes turned into hours. Finally the two bodies stirred. They sat up. My grandfather was seen to help Shu Eng Lei to his feet. The man's face was gray and ghastly. They said not a word to each other. The press conference was abruptly cancelled. Witnesses say Shu Eng Lei was ten years older when he returned to his office than when he left it earlier that day. He never again spoke to the press. He hanged himself soon thereafter, in his state apartment, while watching a video of *Public Execution!* "

"What terrible thing did he see in hell?"

Nyima took a long drink from his canteen. "I don't know," he said. "He never told anyone. Anyway, in all the chaos, the secret police arrested my grandfather and everyone else connected with Shu Eng Lei."

"What happened?"

"He was sent to a reeducation facility, where he died. My grandmother and my mother, and all of his wives and children, they all were taken away as well. There were seven of them. Not all of them survived, but my grandmother, the youngest, befriended one of the guards. My mother was born and raised in the camps.

"Eventually my mother's status was revised and she was sent to do child labor in the sweatshops in Shangdong, separating her from her mother, though she was only six at the time.

"After a while she was reassigned to the night shift and, by day, was sent to the factory manager's house to care for his elderly parents. It was a grueling existence and I suspect he used her cruelly, but she had nowhere to go even if she could have escaped.

"At the age of thirteen she was sold to a Beijing businessman over the telephone by the factory manager's secretary. I have seen the pictures of my mother then. I don't know what price she fetched, but I imagine it was substantial. Very young wives were the fashion in Beijing at the time. He married her and they had seven children, of which I am the seventh.

"So I grew up in a wealthy section of Beijing, and I suppose my parents' marriage was normal enough, considering the circumstances, but in fact the man was a drunk. So, one day I caught him abusing one of my older sisters, and I did him in with a pair of scissors.

"We left the old man dead on the bed while my mother arranged passage for me to Taiwan. The plan was for them to join me later, but in fact I never heard from them again. No doubt they are long dead, arrested and sent to the camps.

"In Taiwan I lived with relatives and studied at Tai-da University. I got my degree in electrical engineering. I have Taiwanese citizenship under a slightly revised version of my Mainland name. I applied for a job as an engineer in a nuclear plant in the hinterlands of Sichuan, far from here. I worked with the safety inspectors on the main reactor. They were all Chinese, and they all thought I was Chinese."

Mila gazed at his inanimate face with growing horror. "Not the power plant disaster! You?"

Nyima nodded grimly. "One night I stayed late at work. I switched the leads on the reactor dampers and disabled the thermostats. It was so simple. The only difficult part was getting away alive. I left the plant and started running. It is very isolated there, in a high desert. There is one road that leads to a village where you can catch a bus. You can bet I waited an anxious time before the next bus arrived. But I guess I got out of there before getting a bad dose, since I am alive."

"How many died?" Mila asked.

Nyima shook his head, as if that were an irrelevant question.

Basang answered for him: "There was heavy loss of life."

"But not all were Chinese," pointed out Dolma. "Nyima is insane, a murderer. Innocent Tibetans died in his insane act of revenge."

"Some died, it is true," sniffed Nyima. "But I blame it all on the Chinese. They should have poured concrete over the entire installation and then spent the next five years hardening the shielding. But did they do that? No, they waited hours while it fizzled out of control and then they evacuated only essential personnel. Of course Tibetans died. The authorities were negligent. That's not my fault, is it?"

Mila licked his lips. "I guess it could be debated."

"Of course it is his fault," muttered Dolma, kneeling by the fire. "That is why he tells the story about hell."

Nyima gave her an irritated look. "Anyway, the bus took me to many little hamlets and mountain villages and finally to New Tibet City. I was negotiating to buy some counterfeit travel documents when I ran into Jamyang here."

Mila looked at Jamyang. "Did you know of this before you enlisted him?"

Jamyang admitted that he had not known. But he had not been terribly upset about it when he found out. "The man is a very skilled technician," he said, "and that erases a world of small imperfections, in my book. Besides, power plants are prime targets for sabotage. Where is the moral dilemma?"

"I will do it again whenever I can get a job in another nuclear plant," Nyima asserted calmly. "It was a snap, do you hear? A child could have done it. I can do it again, if I get the right papers."

"I believe him," said the woman named Sonam. "I have spoken with him about a number of things. He is absolutely without conscience or humanity. He could do anything and not worry about the karmic consequences. He is more frightening to me than any of the Chinese I know."

Mila recognized this woman too, a middle-aged, rather stout person. Her braided hair, tidy *chuba,* and matronly affect contrasted strangely with her earlier homicidal frenzy. As if in recognition of her latent ferocity, Nyima made a small protective motion with his left hand, to ward off the evil eye. He looked at her nervously.

"She is a witch," he confided to Mila. "All these women are witches. Have you noticed that no tuckahoes are left in these woods, and none of those glossy little *lingzhi*?"

The third woman laughed harshly. She was a haggard, painfully thin person who, by the boyish cut of her hair, might have been a nun up to a few months ago. The Freetowners called her Ani-la.

"You speak of toadstools! Yet Nyima is not the only one of us who is insane," she said bluntly to Mila. "Violence has driven us all mad. Sometimes I wish I were back in Narkang Prison, and away from all this killing. At least there I could keep my vows. There I was sheltered and fed. Here I must associate with criminals. I am forced to sleep in the woods and trap squirrels. Do you know, in Narkang Prison I was close to *Kundun*?"

"You saw her in prison?" Mila asked eagerly.

"Several times. I even spoke to her once. That was perhaps my happiest moment in prison."

Mila leaned forward eagerly. "Please tell me about it."

"I said to her, 'How are you dealing with prison life?' And she said to me, 'I take it pretty well, except I miss my man Mila. I really want to fuck him!'"

Mila's mouth fell open. Hot blood rushed to his face, and his stomach felt sick. The others looked down in embarrassment, but Ani-la laughed delightedly.

"He believed me!" she crowed. "Look at him! Look how I hurt him! A real man might strike back, but he is nonviolent. What a little prick!"

"Be quiet, woman!" cried Jamyang. "How can you speak in this way? We are all Tibetan here. Save your venom for the Chinese."

Dolma looked at Mila with sympathy. "Ani-la is not right

in her head," she told him gently. "She has been raped so many times, she takes it out on the men. I should have warned you about her. I am very sorry."

"My head is fine," insisted Ani-la angrily. "It is my pelvic area that burns like fire!"

Mila sighed heavily. "I am sorry for her troubles. Let her lash out at me, if it helps her to feel better. It is not important."

Jamyang glared angrily at the thin woman. "I'd like to feed her to the bears. She has been nothing but trouble since I brought her here."

Ani-la stood with dignity and pointed a wavering finger at Jamyang. Nyima made his protective mudra again. Mila tensed himself for an angry confrontation, but the woman stalked off without a word.

No one spoke. The warm night suddenly seemed a little chilly. Mila sat quietly, examining the storm of emotions that the woman's vicious joke had set off in his mind.

"Are you going to be all right?" asked the matronly Sonam.

"Thank you," said Mila. "I am fine."

"Sonam," suggested Jamyang, "perhaps you could fetch a jug of barley beer for our friend. He seems a little distressed."

"He looks like he has been struck in the head with an axe handle," chuckled Basang, as Sonam rose and went out of the circle of firelight.

"Well, what do you expect?" said a voice from the shadows. "Here is a man who had been sheltered all his life in the shadow of the Dalai Lama. And now he has fallen into reality at last. I feel sorry for him."

Mila peered into the shadows beyond the light. Purpu and Pemba sat silently under the trees. They sat close to each other, not moving. It was the one on the right who had spoken. Mila was put off by his words.

"What did you mean, sir, when you say I have been sheltered? Has your life been so wretched that Narkang Prison is like a shelter?" Mila was ready to measure his own travails against those of any Tibetan.

Purbu inched forward so that his face was in the light. Lit from below, his cheekbones cast pools of shadow over his eyes. His skull was triangular and flattened on top. His hair began far back and was pulled tight. Although he was skeletally thin, creases of flesh lined his forehead. His chin was like two unevenly shaped crab apples bulging out of the bottom of his face and his mouth was a thin slash.

"I think what I am saying is obvious," he explained. "And believe me, I have the most complete respect for **Kundun**. Unlike Basang here, I fully believe that she is the emanation of Chenrezig, just as they say she is. She is an enlightened one, a great being, a compassionate Buddha, an omniscient genius. And that is exactly the trouble with her leadership, do you see?"

"No, I do not see," replied Mila with irritation.

There was a pause as Sonam returned with a jug of *chang*. She handed it to Mayor Jamyang, who took a long drink. Wiping his mouth, he passed it to Basang.

Purbu said, "What exactly do you not see?"

"I do not see why you think I have been leading a sheltered life. I was a monk, involved in politics, all the disasters of the satyagraha movement, then fifteen years in the worst prison in Tibet. So where was the sheltering of which you speak?"

"It has all been a show staged for your benefit. For your liberation, not the liberation of Tibet."

"You are mistaken, my friend. I do not see how you can make this argument."

"Here is what I mean. Our Dalai Lama is no fool. She knows the current situation in Tibet is hopeless, just as it has been hopeless for one hundred and forty years. Political autonomy from the Chinese? Don't make me laugh. Sure, even the Dalai Lama does not think it is possible. But does she give up and lie down? No, the enlightened ones never give up. But it is *your* liberation she is fighting for, my friend, yours and the other satyagrahi—not the liberation of Tibet."

"I do not believe that."

"Look at you—your life has been a masterpiece of compassionate action, love, tolerance, nonviolence . . . hell, you are practically a saint. You glow in the fucking dark, with all your virtue and patience. What better life could you ask for? But what about Tibet? Has Tibet benefited? Not at all."

"But prison . . ."

"Sure. The Chinese build terrible prisons. Worldwide, people have heard of Narkang, it's infamous. What happens? Do you avoid it like normal people? No. You seek it out—the Dalai Lama and her white-robed gang. Did your prison time help our cause? Did it have any impact at all? No. How could it? It was for your own good. You see?"

Mila could not believe what he was hearing. "The starvation, the beatings . . ."

"All very difficult, no doubt, but better than going into the hells, right? Whatever transpires for us humans here on earth, it is bound to be better than the hells, the ghost realms, the insect world. Isn't that what the Buddha proclaims?"

"Yes, it is, but . . ."

"Grow up and face it. She is like all the great ones. She considers individuals, not nations. You are one of the lucky ones, eh? The rest of us do not have such a compassionate guru with such an enlightened overview. We are only biding our time as humans, waiting to go to the hells. Because of our actions in this life, our sufferings there will be unimaginably worse, I trust to that. You, on the other hand, will be spared. You have made passing grades in *Kundun's* nice little school."

"I do not understand you," said Mila. "If you believe what

you are saying, if you believe in the incontrovertible nature of causes and their effects, and in the terrible suffering of the hells, then why do you act violently? Why do you hunt animals? Why do you kill Chinese?"

"Because the strength of my hatred is too much for me. And also I love Tibet."

Nyima leaned over and handed Mila the jug of beer. Not thinking, he took a swig, then another. It was good *chang*.

"I love Tibet also," he said, the beer rising straight to his head. No one answered. Mila shouted angrily: "Do you think I am not a patriot? After all I have been through?" Mila glared at the men and women in the circle. One by one they looked away.

"And what if you are right and I am wrong? What then? Have your violent actions had a better effect? Will Tibet become free because you have killed a handful of Chinese?"

Purbu shrugged his narrow shoulders. "What you say is probably true. We are slaves to our anger. None of us can really do much for Tibet."

"What nonsense," cried Basang. "Tibet will be free. Do not give in to your pessimism."

"And someday bears will march on New Tibet City," said Purbu, smiling thinly.

Mila stared hard at Purbu. "I see what you are saying about the Dalai Lama," he said stiffly. "But I do not believe it. In point of fact, the Buddha himself says the best way to help others is to become enlightened. If that is the case, then this savage anger of yours is of no use to anyone."

"I completely agree," nodded Purbu. "Our anger is our fatal weakness. It will prevent our enlightenment and impel us into lower rebirths. But what can we do? The Chinese are to blame for our rage."

"How can you say that? Doesn't your rage come from within your breast?"

Purbu looked at Mila the way he might regard a naive child. He turned to his brother.

"Pemba, come into the light."

Pemba hesitated for a moment, then edged forward into the light. Mila was again amazed at the sight of two men who looked exactly alike. Pemba's head was a flat-topped triangle. Lines of flesh creased his otherwise thin forehead. His chin bulged unevenly beneath a mouth that was a thin, embittered line.

"You are the first twins I have ever seen," said Mila.

"We are not twins," said Pemba. His voice was identical to Purbu's. "The Chinese do not allow twins. We are clones."

"We were cloned," echoed Purbu. "We had the same Tibetan father in the sense that we came from the same cultured cells. No human mother was needed for us. Originally, we were seven. Hence we were named for the days of the week."

"But the other five were murdered by the Army," Pemba said.

"That is right," said Purbu. "Our brothers were all murdered."

"Sacrificed to Communist science."

"Over a long time, over a period of years."

"For science, you understand?"

"We never knew which of us they would take, or when."

"Those were not the best of times, but we were always a close-knit family, we days of the week."

"It is hard to be two and not seven. We knew each other's hearts. We shared each other's minds."

"It is a fact," agreed Basang. "The brothers will not say so, but they are telepaths. There is no other explanation for the way they hunt."

"Or the way we escaped," chuckled Purbu, drinking *chang*.

"Do you remember the guard's terror when we caught him in our trap?" laughed Purbu.

"It was sweet revenge for us, dear brother."

"And so you see, Mila," said Pemba. "We are different from you. We hate our tormentors."

"I have reason to hate them also," protested Mila.

"Certainly—who does not? But it is your love for *Kundun* that is the core of your being."

Mila held his head in his hands. "This is what we have come to, isn't it?" he asked miserably. "To kill for revenge, with no hope of political advantage. Is this what we have become?"

"Come now," said Mayor Jamyang, putting down the empty jug. "We are all exhausted. We have said many foolish things. We are a band of brave freedom fighters, that is all. Any more is just tiredness."

Jamyang led Mila back to the cave. By the light of the electric torch, Mila could see that the women had repaired the cave. They had even prepared a second roll of bedding for Mila to lie on. He was so tired he could hardly think, and already asleep when he heard Jamyang say, "What the hell happened to my wok?"

5

Mila labored in the rocky field with the other citizens of Freetown. The day was very hot. The ground they turned for the planting of onions lay in a narrow *tang* between two ridges. By early afternoon the high walls would shadow the narrow valley, but now it was almost noon and there was no shade. The heat of the plains below could not be worse than this day's heat. Small winged ants and other pests buzzed and settled on the salty droplets that coursed down their faces, arms, and legs. Their ragged clothes, patched and stained and worn in all seasons, were wet with perspiration. The women had removed their aprons and wrapped them like turbans around their heads.

The earth was sharp with rock and shale that had washed down the cliffs. Not everyone had sandals. Some of the men wrapped their feet with strips of animal skin. All but Mila and the women carried captured Chinese weapons in case of a surprise attack.

They were arrayed across the field, readying the ground for planting. Their hoes and mattocks rose and fell, reminding Mila of the violence he had witnessed in the cave. Song would have made their work go more easily, but instead they worked in discontented silence, with the occasional shout if a large rock was unearthed. Mila plied his mattock. It rose and fell in harmony with the tools of the others, and the piles of rock grew larger, marking their slow progress down the valley. Behind them, small cairns of rock marked their progress. Their Mayor planned to use the rock to build proper latrines.

The women toiled separately from the men, staying far off across the valley floor, over toward the east wall where the rocks were large. The men worked the west. To the north, where the mountain was steep, Basang was climbing a sheer rock face that rose sixty meters to a narrow shelf. Basang had proven himself to be the best climber. He was as athletic as a mountain goat. His mission was to collect the delicate herbs, chamomile, and burdock that grew on the highest hillsides and the hard-to-reach crags.

Not far from the women, by the eastern cliff wall in the shade of an overhang, stood a large leather water bucket. Purbu and Pemba had placed it there before dawn, carrying it between them carefully so that it sloshed very little. A maroon shawl kept off the dust, and a wooden dipper weighed down the shawl.

They had determined to work until noon before drinking the water, but the yellow sun was high and hot and now they were all very thirsty. They began to feel it must be noon. Mila especially was eager to drink; he had not fully quenched the terrible dry thirst that had accompanied him to Freetown. He straightened his aching back, placed his mattock head first on the rocky earth, and glanced longingly at the water.

Jamyang also looked at the water. The ground was uneven there, but less rocky and good for onions. The others noticed that Mila's mattock had ceased its rhythmic chopping, and they stopped their labors also. Suddenly the buzzing of the pests seemed loud. All across the field, the Freetowners were laying down their tools and straightening their spines with a hand to the small of their backs. Grunting, they stretched. Unwinding their makeshift turbans, they mopped the sweat from their arms and legs. Their dust-darkened faces broke into bright smiles.

Across the rocky field, Sonam turned to walk toward the water bucket. Her bare feet were dusty and dark from the sun. Near her, Dolma and Ani-la both wore rubber thong sandals of a make and manufacture recognized by Mila. They were produced in Nar-kang Prison from old tractor tires. They were sensible sandals with good tread and were widely worn throughout Tibet, where even the wearing of a sandal can be a political act.

Sonam took another step. Her right foot struck a small metal knob that protruded above the ground. She had not seen it there; the metal knob was covered with a dusting of wind-blown earth. The land mine detonated in a furious roar of black smoke and red fire.

Sonam was thrown back onto her neck. She lay on the ground just visible through a cloud of black dust, crying in surprise and horror. The beginning of her scream was lost in the roar of the explosion, but it went on and on and mingled with the screaming of the birds of prey who, disturbed by the blast, rose from their perches in the highest hills.

Dolma, standing ten feet from the accident, was frozen with fear. She looked on as Sonam writhed on the ground in agony, whipping her head this way and that and reaching her hands down to her shattered leg. The explosion lifted a cloud of pulverized rock and earth to blacken her skin, and the blackness glistened with gouts of red blood that welled from wounds on her face and chest and arms. Sonam cried out, "Help me! Help . . ." Her voice was thick and forced. "Oh, Lord! Oh, help! My legs!" she cried, and it seemed to the immobilized Mila that she entreated him personally to come to her aid but, really, her eyes had been blinded by the flying debris of the blast. Mila wanted to run to her assistance, but he hesitated in the face of an onion field planted with Chinese mines. The relentless sun beat down hotter than before, but now it was not the heat that caused the sweat to pour down their faces.

Through the din, Ani-la, who was closest to the explosion, cried hoarsely, "Sonam, I'm coming!" But tripping across the broad blade of her hoe, she sprawled forward onto the ground. A muffled blast tore into her chest. She flopped crazily for a moment, then died. Her hand fluttered spasmodically, then closed. The fringed edges of her loosened robe burned with weird green fire.

Mila's heart was in his throat. Ani-la was clearly dead, but Sonam still thrashed on the ground in agony, alternately reaching her hands toward her ruined limbs and holding them out towards her nearest companion. Dolma, however, did not go to her aid. She was in a terrible spot just where she was. It was obvious now that this end of the valley was a killing field. Dolma clearly wanted to run to the assistance of Sonam just as Ani-la had rushed self-lessly to the aid of Sonam. But Ani-la had fallen on a land mine and died. Not only could Dolma not go forward, she could not go back.

None of the men moved an inch.

Slowly, as if unwilling to look at the bearer of unwelcome news, Dolma turned north. Mila followed her gaze, and there on the hillside was Basang.

Basang had wedged himself securely into a cleft in the rock about thirty feet above the valley floor. He had unslung his rifle from his shoulder and was taking careful aim. Mila stared at him in amazement. What the hell was Basang doing? Then the words of Jamyang came back to him with sudden force: "We have a tradition in Freetown. If a man steps on a mine, the others shoot him." Mila's shout—"Basang, no!"—was drowned out by the noise of the rifle shot.

Poor Sonam jerked once and died even before the echo of the report bounced back from the mountain wall. Basang had taken her life accurately. "The consequences are easier to deal with that way," the Mayor had said. Mila shook his head in sorrow. But the consequences of land mines are never really easy to deal with. And now, what was Dolma to do?

The warm summer air was filled with the stench of explosives and blood. The two dead women lay in the smoking field. Bright white shards of Sonam's leg bone—ivory with rivulets of dark red blood—pointed like an accusation at the untouched bucket and the wooden dipper.

Mila looked at Dolma. He felt the horror of her situation. He felt torn by equal measures of compassion and fear. He wanted to move, to go to her assistance, but he was too afraid. *He needed to remain where he was*, for that way he could preserve his own legs, so beloved, his own balls, so dear. His life must be preserved; it was suitable to be cherished. So precious. Still, his compassionate instinct told him to go to Dolma. He wanted to . . . but he could not. In his fear he thought, shamefully, that the others would go. He, Mila, was not the one to walk through the mines. The others had the experience. The others would know what to do.

But Mila was kidding himself. No one was going to walk into those mines to save Dolma. They were safe on the opposite side of the field; their mattocks had already hatched the ground without finding mines. All the mines were on this side, where Dolma now stood, and it was no use hoping there were only a few of them. The Army never put down just a few mines; it deployed them by the hundreds and thousands. Each of the Freetowners knew this, and each of them felt, just as Mila felt—with a surprising newness almost like a pang of adolescent love—that their own feet were precious, their own legs were special, their own lives were of paramount importance.

Mila did not know how to do what he needed to do.

Basang, on the other hand, knew exactly what to do. Up on his perch, he was preparing to shoot Dolma dead, to dispatch her like a horse with a broken leg, so that they could all get on with their business.

Everyone watched Basang's careful preparations. Dolma stood completely still, her hand over her mouth, her eyes closed. She too knew what to do—stand completely still. Let the man with the rifle get the job done.

Mountain triage.

Like the others, Mila could not move, yet he knew now he must help Dolma, and quickly. Basang had already ejected the spent cartridge and loaded another. They had all heard the metallic click-clack; Dolma had flinched very slightly. Now he was sighting down the barrel of the weapon. Mila gathered his courage and uttered a prayer to Lord Buddha. "Guide me through these cursed mines, oh Lord!" he cried with a choked sob. Still he could not move. Then he thought, Lord Buddha, give me Tara Gyatso's strength. I will use it to help Dolma. And holding this thought, although his knees were weak and his stomach churned with fear, he walked straight out into the field toward the dead and the living.

Basang saw him moving and lowered the gun. Jamyang yelled, "Come back, you fool!" but no one else said anything. Mila looked down at the ground in front of him; he did not know if Dolma saw him coming or not. With every step he felt the fear grow large within him, a great ball of dread and nauseating panic. He imagined with every step that he could feel his weight depressing the earth above a hidden detonator, and he expected the roar of the blast and the shock of the explosion, stripping his flesh and shattering his bones, bringing an agony of pain and trauma, and a bullet from the waiting Basang. But he kept on with his prayer, "Lord Buddha, give me Tara's strength," and he continued his terrifying progress toward the woman.

Mila paused at Sonam's body. Hot fragments of land mine had perforated her torso. The sight of her corpse brought tears to

Mila's eyes. He felt a surge of love in his breast that was not directed, so much, toward the dead Sonam, or even toward the imprisoned Tara Gyatso who had lent him her strength, but instead for
all beings who must live and walk among land mines. He prayed
again to Lord Buddha, but his fear did not leave him—instead,
it increased until it burst out beyond the boundaries of his own
mind and became fear for everyone. Now he saw the truth—for
every being there was a land mine. It waited, hidden, just under
the ground. Oh, he could see that now, now that he was in the
middle of the minefield. And in that instant the full measure of
Tara Gyatso's strength became clear to him. It was infinite and joy-
ous. She could do anything. She could clear land mines with her
own limbs until the Communists relented. With reincarnations
limitless in number, she could walk the fields, clearing the mines
one by one with her own feet until there were no more. With her
own limbs. With her myriad lives. Mila's crazy tears became joy-
ous. She was going to clear them all; he saw now that she could.
She would use her limitless strength for just that purpose. Lord
Buddha would smile.

He held out his hand to the astonished Dolma.

6

To Dolma's credit, she remained calm. She took Mila's hand and allowed herself to be led out of the mines past the bodies of her sisters. She held her head high and walked like an aristocrat crossing an acre of manure. Not speaking, she followed him placidly, without even an apprehensive glance at the others, placing her feet daintily where Mila's had been. And when they were safely out of the mines and back among the surviving Freetowners— themselves silent, mouthing prayers or making small superstitious signs in the air—even then she did not collapse into hysteria, but merely sat by the bucket, quite indifferent, it seemed, to her narrow escape, drinking a ladle of water. Mila stood nearby, detached from the scene, breathing heavily and looking at the empty blue sky.

The citizens of Freetown gave both of them a wide circle of privacy. They were afraid to be in the presence of such power, yet proud.

"She is a witch," Basang exclaimed to one and all, when he had climbed down from the hillside and rejoined his friends.

"Mila must be under her spell, one way or another."

"That, or he is the world's great imbecile," conceded Jam-yang, wiping the sweat from his brow with a wild grin.

"Let's ask what got into him."

But Mila had already wandered off. No one tried to stop him, and Dolma seemed not to notice.

Mila walked out of Freetown, away from the field where Sonam and Ani-la lay. He wandered without destination across a range of hills that gradually rose to a high ridge overlooking a long valley. The Freetowners never went down into the valley, suspecting that it had been mined, but the upper reaches of the surrounding hills were lovely, with alpine larch and hemlock woods on the sheltered lower slopes and a grand view off to a somber range of naked granite mountain peaks. Mila came to a meadow with a stream running through it, and followed it uphill to where a small waterfall fell over smooth wet rocks. The water was cold and gritty. He drank until his stomach ached, then sat in a comfortable place in the shade with a good view.

These pine and spruce woods were filled with songbirds with bright plumage that twittered and sang in the trees above Mila. They swooped and dipped to bathe their beaks and wings in the freezing cold water. Mila was not a keen observer of the woods, but now that he made his home in the mountains, he was learning to relax and enjoy the serenity of nature.

Sitting quietly in the shade, Mila appreciated the sounds water made splashing over rock, the fluent murmuring of moving liquid. The branches of the pines reached out and brushed their needles together, creating another sound, a purposeful whisking with an occasional whack.

Small insects buzzed around his face and arms as he sat, and it seemed to him that these high-pitched vibrations were also a language, a way of communicating danger and opportunity, scandal and excitement, fragrant blossoms or rotting fruit.

Mila drowsed in the shade of his tree, hearing the waterfall and the insects hovering around his face and arms, smelling the good smells of the woods, and breathing the clean mountain air.

He felt peaceful—a feeling he had not had in a long time—and the political struggle seemed far away. He felt relaxed and happy, a way he had not felt since the day he had been released from prison.

It was bliss, he told himself. It was complete bliss. I felt the secret power, I felt the magic.

Yes, he told himself, but wasn't that because you missed all the mines? How would you have felt if you had blown off your legs?

Mila had to admit that he would have felt like an ass, lying there in his failure and his agony, waiting for Basang's bullet to end his humiliation.

But I avoided the mines, he thought. I have had my lucky day. Thanks to the Three Jewels, I survived my own great stupidity. Oh, Buddhas and bodhisattvas, prayed Mila, you gave me a fine gift of luck, to save her from Basang's bullet. Now I promise you this: I will never risk my legs with the mines again.

Mila made his promise and he felt much better for having made it. Feeling reassured about his limbs and his future, and enjoying the warmth and the fragrant breeze, Mila dozed. He had not been sleeping long when a noise brought him back to consciousness. He opened his eyes and saw something moving among the trees.

It was not far from where Mila sat—perhaps twenty yards off in the trees on the border of the woods. At first Mila thought it was a Yeti, but looking closer he discerned a large black bear prowling through a stand of mulberry trees. Mila had never seen a bear before. He was surprised at its intimidating size. Moreover, its mouth made frightening sounds, like the gnashing of swords, while just eating fruit.

The bear was in constant motion, stripping branches, chewing up leaves and berries in its fierce jaws, sitting on its haunches, standing to its full height, or walking pitched forward on its four turned-in paws.

Mila did not move, but the breeze on the hillside was variable, and he knew that sooner or later the bear would smell him. And just as he had that disquieting thought, the bear did smell him. It backed away from the trees on its hind legs, pointing its questing muzzle into the air as a hound might do.

Mila had heard that a man might survive an encounter with a bear if he pretended to be a corpse. It was just as well, since he was too afraid to move even a muscle.

The bear, on the other hand, was quivering from its bared teeth to its six-inch-long claws. It dropped to all four legs and began to move with a swaying motion toward the tree where Mila was pretending to be dead. The beast looked directly Mila; Mila looked directly at the beast. Its furious eyes were beady black coals.

The bear moved slowly, lumbering directly at Mila. Too late, Mila also remembered that a man might escape a bear by climbing a tree. Even now, if he could have moved, he might have tried climbing the tree, but he could not move; and since he had never climbed a tree, and had no idea how to accomplish that athletic feat, the bear would probably just pluck him down like an apple.

At ten yards and closing, the bear sighted Mila with his uncertain vision. Seeing that Mila was a man, and having some experience of men and their stings and bangs, he reared up on his hind legs and roared.

Mila leaped to his feet and cried out in terror. Just then it happened with the bear as it had happened with the Chinese corporal. Suddenly, with a strange dislocation, he knew the bear from within. He looked out on the world through the bear's eyes. He could see himself, not in the vivid colors of human vision but through the myopic, panoramic lenses of a bear's eyes. Mila looked down from his great height and saw himself cowering at the base of a tree. From the bear's perspective, the sight of this human was unwelcome. A hairless ape was always dangerous, alone or in a pack. They carried wood and iron, and threw lightning with their magic. They set traps. They planted lightning in the fields, such that any bear walking there was liable to be struck with lightning. It was best to exercise extreme caution in attacking a human, remaining mindful of the creature's cunning.

Mila could look through the bear's eyes and feel the bear's anger and fear, sharing space in the bear's mind as he had with Corporal Jimmy. He could clearly smell the disgusting scent of his human body through the bear's nostrils.

Mila even understood some of the bear's emotional life. The beast was a male, a powerful marauder. He had often heard the humans call him *Dom,* with great fear and respect, so he thought of himself as *Dom.* He was feared throughout the mountains by all the lesser creatures, be they human or puma, eagle, or salmon. Within the circle of bears, he was considered a powerful warrior. It was rare for him nowadays to smell a rival, and his nearest neighbor carefully stayed ten foraging days from the center of *Dom's* marked territory. With the she-bears he was hell on paws. *Dom* was a formidable stud with a highly evolved nose. The merest scent of a she-bear thickened his balls to the size of coconuts. In his day, *Dom* had mounted the most beautiful-smelling females between Ladakh and Shigatze, sometimes following his throbbing member for weeks in a lust-induced beeline straight to the dripping, reeking, swollen cunny of some snarling, dangerous, highstrung brunette. Oh, the slashings he had endured for love!

Dom was a religious bear as well as a lover. As the most superior of mountain beings with no natural predators, it was his duty to propitiate the most powerful spirits. He was the priest of lightning from above and lightning from below; of fire, famine, drought, and flooding. The males in the circle depended on him never to forget his responsibility to the world of shades—to the old ones gone beyond, to the little ones yet to come, to the Others, whose ancient smells were nearly gone. He was, in truth, a complex being, and a bear worthy of respect, and Mila was willing to respect him greatly, but Mila could also see that *Dom's* primary mode of response was savage aggression.

And just at that moment the beast dropped again to all fours and began to move forward. Try as he might, though Mila could experience the bear's world from deep within him, there was nothing he could do to stop the bear from attacking.

Mila smoothly exited the bear, returning to his own heart and mind. *Dom* was directly on top of him. Mila yelled:

"*Om mani padme hung!*"

The bear ceased his forward motion for the space of a heartbeat. Mila looked into the animal's slavering jaws and remembered the big bear's name. He reached out an arm and pointed his finger at the beast. "Hai! *Dom!* Go back!"

In retrospect, this was regrettable. The bear struck open-clawed at Mila's outstretched arm, breaking the ulna and radius with tremendous force and slicing deep into the muscle with razor-sharp claws. The impact spun Mila back into the tree, breaking his collarbone and dislocating his shoulder. The bear struck with the other paw, cutting into Mila's ribs and sending him flying into the freezing cold water of the stream. Mila plunged head first onto the water-covered stones, banging his already injured ribs. The water ran red.

Mila struggled to get to his knees, but he was driven down into the streambed by a tremendous weight. The hot fur of the bear smothered Mila's efforts to rise, and for a second he could smell the peculiar sweet and sour reek of the bear. Then he felt hot breath on his neck and head and the bear's teeth clamping down hard on either side of his skull. Goodbye, he thought, as the bear bore down, teeth scraping down the sides of his head seeking more purchase, grinding Mila's nose and lips and chin into the large and small stones at the bottom of the stream.

Goodbye, Mila thought again, and at that precise instant the bear relaxed his grip on Mila's skull and moved out of the water and up the bank, relieving Mila of his tremendous weight. The bear sauntered off, apparently with total indifference to Mila. He lay where he was as long as he could, then rolled over onto his side and dragged his saturated body out of the water. The bear was ambling away among the mulberry trees. Mila dragged himself painfully up onto the bank until his legs were out of the water. Each breath caused a flash of pain in his side. He looked down at his mangled arm. It looked very bad. There was a steady flow of blood. "The arm needs a tourniquet," he muttered to no one in particular. Lacking the initiative to tie one himself, he blacked out. A short while later he opened his eyes to see three faces from Freetown staring down at him with grave concern. "By the gods, he lives!" exclaimed one of them.

Mila had survived the attack of the bear, but only by a small margin. He also survived the trek back to camp, where he was conveyed by a hastily built travois, but also just barely.

Dolma, the most accomplished healer in Freetown, had him brought into her narrow cave. She laid him on the blankets where Sonam had bunked. The other Freetowners stood anxiously around the entrance. It was now their firmly held belief that Dolma and Mila *both* were skilled magicians, powerful sorcerers who could make deals between the king of the underworld and the god of bears. How else explain the fact that Mila had walked boldly off across the minefield to rescue the witch and then went immediately into the woods to keep his appointment with *Dom*? What appalling bargain had he struck with the Powers? More proof that Mila was a powerful magician. Freetown was fortunate—it was most auspicious—to have two such powerful yogis among the people. The men had always prized the women for their shamanic ability to keep away bears, and Mila's ability to strike supernatural bargains—negotiating his own limbs for the life of another—was bound to yield advantage somehow.

Meanwhile, Dolma continued to demonstrate her mastery of the healing arts by exposing and cleaning her man's wounds, treating them with layers of healing herbs, and bandaging them with the cleanest rags to be found in Freetown, soaked in spirits of wine. She set his broken arm as best she could, but the arm was crushed and mauled. There was no painkiller apart from the wild mountain herbs, so she made a tea for him from the buds and flowers. As she changed the dressing late that night, while Mila slept, she sniffed the wounds one after the other, smelling the mauled arm with the concentration of a connoisseur. The next morning, when Mayor Jamyang entered the cave to bring her another armful of bandages, she asked him in an undertone to accompany her outside.

"What is it, Dolma?" he asked when they were out of Mila's hearing.

Dolma smoothed her hands on her multi-colored apron. "I will be needing a few things," she said simply.

The Mayor nodded expectantly. "Cushions, bandages, perhaps some tasty soup?"

"I need a short length of wood, perfectly round and straight. I want it peeled and smooth. It must be perfectly peeled and completely smooth. About four inches in diameter. The lower bough of a birch tree should suffice."

The Mayor was pulled up short. "A length of wood . . . ?"

"And I need for you to sharpen and then boil your butcher knife. Do you hear me, Mayor? It must be boiled for at least an hour. When it has cooled, do not touch it with your bare hands." She glanced sharply at his grubby outdoorsman's hands. "If you do, it will kill him."

The Mayor's eyes became wide. "Are his wounds that bad?" he asked. Dolma dismissed his question with a sideways flick of her wrist.

"And listen," she said quickly. "I also will require . . . " She

whispered her needs to the horrified Mayor. When she \
the Mayor glanced at her sharply, then bowed and backe
from her cave. Dolma stood for a moment looking out o
sunlit valley, her eyes the merest slits. Whenever Mila strug͚ ͺu
against the bear in his sleep, the wounds reopened and he cried
out in pain. She was listening.

Later that day and into the night, when Mila became inured
to the effects of the hemp, there was no other drug to dull the
pain. The awful pain itself was the only drug. It scattered his wits
and limited his awareness. Mila could hear what was going on
around him, but it was as if he was asleep while listening to radio.
Since he had never actually heard a radio program in Tibetan, it
was at least a novel experience. From time to time the novelty of
it caused him to surface into a shallow pool of consciousness, but
the intense pain at this clearer level drove him deep again. When
he could not submerge into the deeper levels of his mind through
suffering alone, he tried meditation.

As a young monk, Mila had trained in the debate courtyards
to be a Geshe. He studied the great topics of Tibetan scholarship,
and he practiced ritual and meditation. His favorite meditation
was selflessness yoga. In selflessness yoga, one isolates one's illuso-
ry sense of self and examines it to determine where the self might
reside. The skilled yogi looks for the self among the constituents
of body and mind, outside the body and mind, as the owner of
the constituents, as their collection, and so forth. Not finding an
independent self in any of these ways, the yogi experiences real-
ization and is released from suffering. Mila had often practiced
selflessness yoga. Now, in his bed of pain, he applied himself to
it again. Unfortunately for Mila, a clear mind is required for the
analysis, and Mila slid in and out of delirium. The only aspect of
the meditation he could focus on involved determining that the
self is not the owner of the aggregates. He could vaguely remember that there were two aspects to this: one could own something

in the sense of a man owning a cow, and one could own in the sense of a man owning his own head. But what was it about owning his own head? Did he own his own head or not? In his delirium he had a vision of himself, the owner of his head, complete with a head, and also of the head that was owned—a second head. In Mila's fever-induced dream, he was carrying this second head, and due to his ability to project his consciousness, sometimes he looked out of the eyes of one head, sometimes the other. Back and forth, back and forth.

"Back and forth, back and forth," he murmured through his clenched teeth and blackened lips. "Owner of the cow, owner of the head . . ." Over and over he repeated his litany, as Dolma knelt by his side and tended his wounds with infinite care. She had not the slightest idea what was going through his mind. But after a while Mila's mutterings grew weak, and his words indistinct. In his dreams he saw himself as a proud lion prowling through a forest of snow-covered ferns, or swimming in a bowl of delicious yogurt, or standing beside his own head, or collapsing in on himself, or existing as a million miniscule Milas, a monstrous swarm of particle-Milas, creating the shape of a man where there was no man.

After his delirium had run its course, his sufferings returned. As Dolma knelt over his sweating, tormented body, Mila suddenly could stand the pain no more and, with an effort of will, projected his consciousness up and out of his body, flinging it across the gap between his own heart and the external world, until . . .

. . . he was free again, suddenly free from the pain-wracked bondage of his human form. Mila found himself in the body of a falcon, a cold-minded bird of prey, circling high above a large gathering of birds in a field where the dead bodies of two humans lay swollen from the heat.

Tactical Area One was a boon to carrion birds and rodent predators. The one could fly above the devices, the other could scurry right over them without depressing the detonators. This falcon knew the whereabouts of every killing field in these central highlands, and it patrolled them for birds and rodents each day.

The falcon could soar for hours without effort. Mila had never experienced the thrill of flight except during his drainpipe dreams, when he had shared the mind of a dove. The falcon's eyesight was of an extreme resolution that the myopic Mila had never imagined possible. He could sense the slightest movement on the mountaintops and hillsides far below. The bird's eye for detail from this height was nothing short of wonderful, and the bird's memory was also finely detailed. Although Mila enjoyed the sensation of flight, finding the thermal currents and riding the updrafts, he did not enjoy the bird's terrifying power dives and sudden, violent kills.

While Mila shared in the experience of the falcon as it flew in lazy loops above the minefield, Jamyang the Mayor returned to his own cave. Basang and Nyima were squatting on their haunches. In front of them was a cloth-wrapped bundle. Around them stood a small crowd of men. Men in quilted jackets mixed with bare-armed men in furs and kilts, and others in traditional dress, with long sleeves that flowed from shoulder to ankle. They all looked grim.

"What is it?" Jamyang asked Basang.

Basang pulled a soldier's rifle from its cloth wrap. "Look what we found in the Ani-la's cave. An automatic rifle. PLA issue."

"And two belts of ammo," added Nyima, with a significant look.

"Really? In the Ani's cave?" Jamyang was astonished. "Where the hell could she have gotten such an armory?"

"Sonam and Ani-la shared the cave. It could have been Sonam's," admitted Basang. "Seems more likely to me the Ani had the gun, that's all."

"Neither of them had a weapon when I brought them in,"

Jamyang observed. "No way they could have concealed these." He took the weapon from Basang and turned it over in his hands.

"It is a fine weapon," he pronounced, looking around at the men. "Fully automatic, eight point seven em-em, laser sight, collapsible stock . . ."

The men all nodded. They had already appraised the rifle.

"What we want to know was how it came to be in Sonam's possession," reiterated Basang. "What the hell, Jamyang? Was she planning to kill us all in our sleep?

"Now, boys . . ."

Just then a young man with shifty eyes and a sallow face stepped forward through the crowd of men. His name was Dawa. He had a crushed felt hat in his hands, and he was turning it round and round. He cleared his throat.

"What is it, Dawa?" asked Jamyang, surprised to see the taciturn youth stepping up to speak.

"Well, um, Mayor. Yesterday I come across a dead Red under some bushes on the next hill over." Dawa paused meaningfully.

"Go on."

"That is to say, I come across most of him. Some of him was missing. He was chopped up most awful. Looked like some sort of butcher knife done the job. Maybe numerous different knives. Then he was dragged out into the hills by the heels. I followed the track back to Freetown, clear as paint. Sure as hell he was killed here."

"Weapons?"

"Not a thing on him."

The men exchanged significant glances. Now it was clear to them what had happened to the Chinese soldier: he had been ambushed one way or another by the women of Freetown. "Maybe numerous different knives," the boy had said. Jamyang in particular was a thinking man. He had no trouble connecting the dead soldier and the ruined wok and the butcher knife that now needed sharpening.

"Poor bastard." Jamyang shook his head. "I guess he didn't have a chance with the gentle ladies of Freetown."

"Which they also cut off his prick," added Dawa.

Jamyang the Mayor sighed. "I was thinking of going into the city to find more women," he said to Basang, "but maybe I will put that off until spring."

"Spring is a good time to travel," agreed Basang, rolling his eyes.

Then the Mayor glanced sharply at Dawa. "Why didn't you tell us about this soldier yesterday, boy?"

"Well, sir." Dawa averted his gaze from the Mayor. "I didn't tell nobody cause I nicked the feller's boots." The young man displayed his PLA mountain footgear amidst general laughter from the men, several of whom wore identical boots. But Jamyang did not laugh and continued his scrutiny of the young man.

"Now son," Jamyang said patiently, "you see that we all steal their boots. I doubt you would scruple over a thing like a pair of boots. It seems to me you must have nicked something more interesting, or you would have told us about the soldier yesterday. Now tell old Mayor Jamyang—what else did you take from that corpse?"

"I . . . I didn't take nothin' else. So help me!"

Basang turned his cold marksman's eyes on the lad. "Tell us what you nicked, Dawa, or . . . "

The threat went unuttered, but the youth turned pale. The other men muttered menacingly and closed in their circle. It was very bad form in Freetown not to share and share alike.

Dawa saw that he was found out.

"All right," he said, "all right. It weren't much of nothing." He reached into a pocket. "There was just this one other thing. But it don't work." And so saying, he produced a black plastic handheld block of electronics with a screen, now blank. The men regarded the device in silence.

"Standard Army issue," nodded Basang, as though he had known it all along.

"I figured it was a cell phone," Dawa continued nervously. "Thought I could sell it in town."

Jamyang the Mayor snorted. "You could have lost your fingers fooling around with that gadget. The little devils blow up."

"They does?" Dawa looked at it with horror.

Basang laughed at his discomfort. "What of theirs doesn't blow up? Fucking Reds!"

"Show it to Nyima," said Basang, jerking his head towards his companion. "Nyima is our electronics expert."

Nyima took it carefully. He examined it as if it were already ticking. "There is Chinese on the back. It says, 'Hand-held Tactical Positioning and Communications Short-Wave Device, Property People's Liberation Army.' Serial number. Unauthorized Use Forbidden." Nyima looked around at the men. "This is a fucking gold mine," he said. "This is better than an alpha-sniffer. But we need the password."

"Dawa, take Nyima to see the body of this corporal. Perhaps he can find a clue to the password."

Nyima rose to his feet, taking the mapping device. "I'll see what I can do. If I make any guesses as to the password, I'll get Dawa here to punch them in."

"What? Not me!"

"It is your punishment for being a damned thief," said Jamyang the Mayor. "Now go. I must sharpen the chopping knife that was blunted on the bones of this soldier. Our gentle Dolma plans to remove Mila's arm."

"It is Mila's quit-price for the life of the witch," said Basang darkly, as the men filed out.

"Let us not speak of that. Please light the fire. I need to boil this hatchet. Now that I think on it, I will boil it twice."

Basang rose to gather sticks. The motion of a distant bird

caught his eye. "It is a Saker falcon," he said with pleasure. "They are coming back to these hills, thanks to the minefields."

7

Dolma spent most of that day quietly cleaning the floor of the cave around Mila's bed. She brought in dried straw, boiled rags, and old sheets of Chinese propaganda posters and laid them down in careful layers. Dolma wished there was another woman left in Freetown capable of helping her amputate Mila's arm, but Sonam had been the only nurse. The men would not be the slightest help. Jamyang the Mayor had a good head on his shoulders, but she doubted that even he had the stomach for what had to be done now. He might puke onto the floor of the cave, spoiling all her sanitary precautions. As for the others, they were convinced that Mila and Dolma were magicians, and would not even enter the cave.

Later that afternoon, Jamyang the Mayor brought the sharpened knife wrapped in a clean old flannel shirt. He also brought a newly peeled birch log that was straight and clean—as fine a piece of hardwood as Dolma could have wished. He also brought a shoulder bag filled with ritual appurtenances from Ani-la's cave. Dolma looked at it for a while, and then at Mila's arm. She had a dilemma. She was experienced enough as a nurse to realize that Mila's broken and mangled arm could not be saved. She also thought it likely that she could successfully remove the arm at the shoulder joint, just as she had seen her father do with the legs of butchered sheep. But the sheep had been dead, and thus cooperative. Mila was unconscious now, but she was sure that at the first touch of the blade he would spring to awareness. How could she hold him still?

Dolma decided to wait until Mila awoke. She was tormented by her decision, but she did not have the strength to operate on an unwilling patient. Still, if she waited too long, the gangrene would spread. In that case Mila would not survive with or without the arm.

The rest of the day went slowly. Mila was resting well: he raved only a little as his infection spread. Dolma feared the rising fever. Mila was being worn down by his pain and injuries. But towards mealtime, Mila awoke from his sleep refreshed and cheerful. He took water, raved very little, complained not at all, and seemed genuinely grateful to Dolma during his lucid moments.

He was a delight to nurse, and Dolma found herself praying over his arm in a way that would have convinced the men that she was a witch, had they needed further convincing.

On the morning of the next day he seemed alert enough to consume a broth made from venison. But his arm was now swollen and discolored, causing great pain, and the smell was terrible. Dolma could wait no longer. She leaned over his bed and spoke solicitously but directly:

"Mila, I am afraid that your injured arm has become infected. Gangrene is setting in. I am sorry to tell you that I will have to act quickly now to remove it."

Mila nodded slowly. His face was waxen and slightly gray with pain and stubble.

"I am very sorry to put you through all this trouble," he said, carefully articulating his words. "I am fortunate to be in the hands of such an accomplished doctor."

Dolma said nothing in answer to that—it was best that the patient have confidence in the abilities of the doctor.

"I am afraid that we have no anesthetic," she said gravely. "We will have to operate while you are conscious."

Mila looked at her in wonderment. He even managed a small ironic laugh. "The wheel of sharp weapons, isn't it?" he murmured.

"All is ready. Let us wait no longer."

Mila closed his eyes wearily. "By all means," he said. "Wait no longer."

"Mila, first I need to position the . . . " Dolma almost said *cutting board*, but decided instead on "foundation." She had the thick piece of peeled wood in her hands. "I have to place this under your arm. It will raise your shoulder for the procedure."

"All right." Mila's voice was a hoarse whisper.

Dolma took the piece of birch wood in one hand, placed her hand under Mila's bandaged biceps, and lifted.

Mila's scream was loud and involuntary. Although he had been interviewed long and often by torturers, he had never experienced any pain like this horrible bolt of agony. His eyes jutted from their sockets and his vision went gray. Unable to control himself, he thrashed away from Dolma and ended up lying partly on his side, panting like a dog and sweating rivulets. His arm and shoulder felt as if they had been bathed in fire.

Dolma quickly removed the piece of wood and eased Mila onto his back. The bandages around his arm were wet and dark. For a moment neither of them spoke.

"That did not go as well as I had hoped," said Dolma quietly.

"Merciful Buddha!" gasped Mila, still panting. "I wish that *Dom* had torn the arm off and been done with it."

"Who?" asked Dolma, puzzled. "Oh, you mean the *dom* who attacked you."

"Yes," said Mila vaguely. "He thinks of himself as *Dom*." He took long, slow breaths.

"But how . . . ? How do you know what the bear thinks?"

Mila was resting more easily now. He tried to explain as Dolma removed the bandages to look at the bleeding.

"I am not sure how, but it has been happening since before I came to Freetown. I spent a few days in a drainpipe without water. My mind became a little deranged. It wandered. It seemed to wander into other places, other creatures. I thought it was just delirium, but since I have been here in Freetown it has happened again, more than once. For instance, I . . . *hunggg*!!"

"Sorry," Dolma apologized. She was cutting the bandage away from his flesh. "Please go on with your story. I will be more careful."

"For instance," Mila resumed, "I knew the Chinese soldier you"—*hacked to pieces*—"dispatched. His nickname was Jimmy. He loved the Chengdu discos. He had a favorite whore." Mila thought for a second. "Named Lulu. I rather liked him."

Dolma looked startled. "But you struck him with the knife. We heard him scream."

"But I could not kill him. I knew his mind too intimately. The enemy must be other."

Dolma sniffed. "I thought of him as a perfect receptacle for all negative feelings. He was intrinsically evil."

"I could not think of him that way, not after looking through his eyes."

Dolma was quiet for a moment, staring at Mila.

"I have heard of the ability, of course," she began dubiously. "The adepts call this practice 'Projection Yoga.' In your case it is different than the Corpse Projection that so famously allowed Marpa's son Dharma Dodey to escape death. Tell me, how often has it happened to you?"

"A few times; and also in dreams."

"To dream of projection is not unusual. But you say you actually *switched* consciousness with the soldier?"

"It was not a switch, so much. It was rather that my part entered his part. I shared in the resources of his head, and of mine."

"That is curious. Your ability seems more innate than learned."

"I was a monk," said Mila self-righteously.

"Some monk," she sniffed. "What else?"

"Well, there was the onion field that day. The land mines. You looked like you needed some help."

"*Some* help?" laughed Dolma. "I was saying goodbye to the world when I felt your hand on mine." She gazed at Mila with moist eyes.

"Yes, I thought you needed some help," continued Mila. "So I asked for some of Tara Gyatso's courage. And I got it."

"I think rather it was your own courage," insisted Dolma, with a hot flush and a tone of jealousy that Mila had seen and heard before but did not recognize in time.

"No, no. I do not have that sort of courage," he assured her. "When it comes to land mines, I am the great coward of Tibet. It was . . . a transference, if you like . . . from Tara Gyatso's mind into mine."

"Hmm. What else?"

"Then came *Dom* the bear. Just before he attacked me, I leaped across the gap into his mind. I knew his bearness, I liked his reek. He was not such a bad fellow, but he was deeply suspicious of humans. There was nothing I could do to stop him from attacking me."

"Have there been others?"

"Just one. The other day—yesterday?—the arm was throbbing. Instead of just lying there in pain, I projected my mind upward into a bird. Medium-sized falcon. Amazing bird! Great wingspread. Solitary glider, like all of them, alone all day with only the sound of the wind in his feathers. Weasels are the juiciest. Did you know that birds divide creatures into beaks and jaws? To a falcon the earth is a giant egg, evident from the way it constantly looms upward on the horizon. Some day soon it may hatch, ending this world and beginning another." Mila realized he was gabbling his words. He had begun perspiring heavily. Now he lapsed into exhausted silence.

Dolma wiped his brow with a wet cloth. "What is paradise, to a falcon?"

"That is easy. Gentle updrafts and fat weasels."

"His concerns are of course important to him."

"Human, bear, falcon: we are all strangely alike. I feel the familiar in all their minds—and the unfamiliar, too. Dolma, do you think I am losing my mind?"

"Well, that is a definite possibility, Mila," Dolma nodded thoughtfully. "Considering what you have been through, in another man I would not entirely rule it out. But probably not you. Perhaps you have propensities for it from a past life, who knows?"

Mila found himself looking carefully into her smiling black eyes. Dolma continued her rumination:

"As it happens, I too know a little something about magic. I have often visited the yogis and magicians in the hills. Yours is a remarkable attainment without training. I strongly advise you not to use it overmuch until we find you a teacher."

"Do you know of one?"

"I do, but not in this neck of the woods. But perhaps I can help you myself. When I was younger, I nursed an old Bon-po *Lopon* magician who taught me the proper rituals for all the yogas. I am not an adept, but I remember the rites."

"But meanwhile I should stop these projections?"

"Definitely. One day you might find yourself trapped with no way back."

"Yes, I see. That is a bad risk to take."

Dolma gazed at his ruined arm thoughtfully.

"But, Mila—perhaps you should risk the projection one more time."

"One more time. You mean . . . ?"

"If you can leave your body for just a short while, I can perform the necessary surgery on your arm."

Mila nodded thoughtfully. "I will try it," he said.

"How will you do it?"

Mila frowned. "It is not so easy to explain. At first the projections were propelled by panic, without any conscious impulses on my part. I did not direct my mind to enter another; as least, I do not remember doing so. Now, however, I have become more familiar with the process. I try to direct it."

"How do you do that?"

"With the falcon, the pain helped—it is easiest when there is plenty of pain, but I cannot exactly say why. Here is what I did: first, I imagined I was bathing my injuries in a cold mountain stream. I examined the extent of each injury. I focused on them, you see?" Dolma nodded. "I let the pain dissolve into the water. When all the pain was in the water, it drifted away down stream. I no longer had the pain, you see? It was all in the water."

"So you felt no pain?"

"I felt it, but it was in the water. It had emptied out of me, or maybe I had emptied out of it. I held it away as long as I could. Then, just before I knew the pain was about to return, I flew into the mind of the falcon. I do not know how it works."

"Increase in concentration, perhaps?"

"Maybe motivation. I do not know. But I would be unable to have such a successful outcome without the pain."

"It seems that you are employing pain for the purposes usually supplied by ritual. Perhaps the proper rituals will replace the need for the pain."

Mila smiled faintly. The sight of his damaged teeth broke Dolma's heart. But the smell of rotting flesh was becoming strong in the hot cavern lit by firelight. "We must hurry," she murmured, raising a bowl of water to his dry lips.

"I am confident," he assured her, raising his head weakly to drink. "I will bathe in the running water; I will fly to the falcon. And when I return, you will have whipped off this old arm and put on a nice new bandage." He nodded complacently.

Dolma took his hand in her fingers and squeezed gently. "You make it sound so good, I look forward with anticipation to our next meeting."

Mila closed his eyes.

Dolma waited. It was not long before there were signs that Mila's mind was gone, his body rigid and cold, his eyes rolled upwards in their sockets. Dolma squeezed his hand tenderly. Tears fell from her eyes onto her bloody apron. Overhead a falcon sailed through the clear evening sky. She picked up the piece of birch wood and positioned it just so.

In the weeks that followed, Mila's wounds recovered more quickly than his spirits. His despair over the amputation of his strong right arm burdened his heart. What good was a maker of crutches with only one arm? He thought often of the child named Dorje and the many others who needed his services. Sometimes it was too much for him, and in his weakened condition, he broke down and cried. On these occasions Dolma was there to comfort him, hug him tenderly, and wipe the tears from his hairy cheeks. She insisted, wisely, that he not think of his life in terms of his past, but rather imagine a brilliant and useful future. A clever man could do a lot of good, she assured him, with one good arm, especially considering that Mila was left-handed.

Eventually, Mila's increasing physical strength erased his despondency. Dolma's tender ministrations forged a bond of intimacy between them. She allowed him no visitors for fear of infection. At night the cave was warm with firelight and incense. By day there was a large fire for boiling water and a smaller fire for the meaty *tukpa*. Dolma's hands became painfully raw from washings in hot water, as thrice daily she bandaged his stump. Dolma made a sweet ritual of the bandaging, fixing her hair, smoothing her apron, making certain that her nursing was accompanied by smiles and laughter. The strain of this playacting was taking its toll, especially since she lay on the hard floor next to him at night and it was hard for her to sleep. Sometimes when he dozed, she would step out into the cool darkness and gaze up at the crystal stars and the moon that her papa called rabbit-keeper, and let herself succumb to the fear that the deadly green infection might return.

But the infection did not return. Instead, Mila slowly recovered from his injuries, and even his troublesome scalp wounds began to heal. These at least were easy to tend, for Mila now boasted a shaved head, his first since leaving the monastery so many years ago.

Dolma lived alone with him in the cave all this time, feeding him, bathing him, changing his bandages, and re-dressing his wounds, which itched furiously—a very good sign of healing. Although it was hard work, Mila was the best of patients . . . never complaining, always cheerful. Except when Dolma forced him to drink large quantities of the herbal tea she prepared for him containing burdock and lemongrass. Mila protested that it tasted horrible and, moreover, caused him to urinate frequently. Dolma attended to this as well as all other aspects of his care. One day, after Mila had regained a portion of his strength, Dolma's ministrations left him sexually aroused. Dolma regarded him shrewdly; then, before either of them knew what was happening, she threw off her clothing and mounted Mila's loins. Mila reached up with his left arm and stroked her breast and flanks. Dolma brought them both to orgasm with long, competent strokes, like an oarsman rowing a boat quickly to the dock.

Mila was surprised at this development, but grateful for Dolma's healing hands. It was a long time since he had had real human contact. As they had saved each other's lives, there was no guessing what further twists their karma might take. Becoming lovers seemed the only normal development that had befallen either of them. But Dolma, of course, had been Mila's—body and soul—since the moment he walked across the minefield and took her hand.

Their physical relationship was tender but unabashed, as sex often is between an injured man and his nurse. Yet between bouts of lovemaking they were shy with one another, without much to say that was not related to Mila's bandages or his wounds. Mila often slept, and Dolma sometimes slept beside him. Outside, the world went its own way without them, and Mila, recovering from his surgery, did not go voyaging with his falcon but stayed with Dolma, who cooked thick broth and sometimes sang.

Meanwhile, Mila was now able to get out of bed and stand up for increasingly long intervals. At first his head swam as if the earth was revolving around him. He also felt lopsided and disconcerted without his arm. His initial attempt to circumnavigate the space in the cave resulted in his veering directly into an outcropping of rock, severely bruising his unprotected ribs on the exposed right side. When the pain subsided, he reversed his directions so as to bang into obstacles with the left side of his body, protected by an arm. Gradually, he was able to compensate for the spinning in his head and his tilt to the left, and soon he was able to walk around the small cave without assistance from Dolma.

One day, while Mila was gingerly pacing around the cave, Dolma ostentatiously removed every article of her clothing and positioned herself on her hands and knees before him. Surprising herself beyond imagining, she wiggled her ruddy, dimpled backside in his direction. Mila was almost as surprised as Dolma. He squinted down at her appealing nakedness for one or two beats of their hearts while the world stood still. Then he loosened his own clothing and knelt behind her. Steadying himself with his one remaining palm, he entered her easily.

The lovers soon found an even, steady rhythm that pleased them both. Their juncture produced a blissful nonawareness of externals. They were like mountain climbers involved in the exertion and beauty of their sport, forgetting, if only for a few moments, the world laid out below them. Enrapt in their own pleasant feelings, they led each other up a series of steep switchbacks to a sudden expansive view of a mountaintop so beautiful they both cried out with pleasure. The high altitude of the summit left them gasping for breath.

Following their lovemaking, Dolma helped Mila onto his back before the fire. She nestled in his arm and for a while glowed and purred with the aftereffects of physical love while Mila, quite pleased with himself, considered falling sound asleep.

Dolma could have slept, as well. The fire was delightfully warm on her skin. Dolma's skin was very sensitive, especially this night. During their sex, she believed that she could feel Mila's eyes wandering over her back and bottom. She could feel a tingling in her skin as if his eye consciousness had somehow warmed her there. It was as if her very skin had finally come awake. She dozed a little in her contentment and, half asleep, felt vividly that she could see downward through the animal skins on which they lay, and that the earth had become the sky, and that the sky went on forever—and somehow she took this as a promise from the gods to her—that Mila would be her man forever.

Mila said mildly into her ear:

"Dolma, have you heard of phantom pain and phantom sensation?"

"What do you mean, my dear?" she asked cozily.

"Sometimes after a person has lost a limb, it still seems to exist. It sends information about how it is feeling back to the heart."

"I do not understand."

"Well, I once made a crutch for a fellow who had suffered for a long time with a swollen knee joint. The mine he stepped on happened to take that leg instead of the other, for which he was very grateful. Anyway, he assured me that he could still feel the swollen knee. On days when the weather was damp, it gave him considerable pain. Even months after the leg was gone."

"Oh, yes. Do you have pain, my dear Mila?"

"No, not pain. I have not felt any phantom pain. But just now, during our, um . . ."

"Yes?"

"When normally I would be using both hands to, well . . ."

Dolma raised herself on an elbow with wide eyes. "Yes? And so?"

"What I am trying to say is, I distinctly felt that I was gripping your exceptionally pleasant posterior with both my hands."

Dolma looked stunned. "I cannot believe I am hearing you say that, Mila. Because, do you know, I vividly felt both of your hands on my flesh. I did not want to say anything because I was afraid you might think . . ."

"This is a phenomenon indeed," smiled Mila. "It seems that my phantom arm has returned to life to engage with us in our lovemaking. You know," he said with a flash of typically Tibetan dark humor, "this could be good news for those who have lost their manhood in war."

Dolma laughed huskily and rolled over to cover Mila's nakedness with her own. "Luckily you have not lost your manhood, my darling; only your arm. And now let us invite it back for another ménage-à-trois," she said with a wicked smile. "I am quite excited by having your phantom arm in the bed with us." And she began to demonstrate that delightful fact to Mila.

Not many days later, when Mila was becoming strong and could sit outside the cave in the slanting sunlight, Dolma left him alone for the morning—for the gathering of botanicals—and not long after she had left, Jamyang the Mayor came strolling by his rock. They greeted each other affectionately.

"Getting along well, I see? Splendid! Splendid!" said Jamyang in the false hearty tones a well man uses toward the sick. "By the way, Mila, I have a little trinket to show you. It's a PLA map device that our boy Dawa took off a corpse. Ever seen one before? It tells your position and displays it on a map, and much more besides."

Jamyang showed the inert plastic device to Mila.

"I don't believe I have ever seen one," said Mila, regarding it with interest.

"Right, the Chinese guard them with their lives, as well they might. Tactical maps—troop positions, minefields, armor, guns." Jamyang's eyes narrowed. "Mila, it turns out our own damned women killed this poor soldier! It is true! They killed him and cut him up horrible. And then to top it, they hid his body in the hills."

"They say the female is more dangerous than the male," said Mila mildly.

"I admire their spirit; I admire it, I admit. But I might expect to be informed. As it was, we were damned lucky Dawa found that body before the Chinese did. And with this map device, we could make some very telling sorties. Get them coming and going. Hit them where it hurts. Unfortunately . . ."

"What, Mayor?"

"Unfortunately the thing requires a password. Without a password, it will surely blow up if we fiddle with it. Oh, well. No use dreaming. But it would have been useful to have their coordinates. Too bad the gals killed that soldier so dead. The twins would have gotten the password out of him. I tell you, those twins frighten the living piss out of Chinese. Hell, they frighten *me*."

Mila took the heavy plastic device in his hand. "So this thing knows where land mines are buried?" he asked incredulously.

"Sure as Buddha has big ears it does. It could tell us the location of the major minefields, safe passage through them, maybe even individual mine placement."

Mila turned the device over and over in his increasingly dexterous hand. "It belonged to a Chinese corporal, you say?"

"That's right." Jamyang the Mayor regarded Mila expressionlessly.

"The keyboard is in Roman."

"Why, sure. You can't have a Chinese keyboard on a little thing like this."

"But the files will be in Mandarin. You read Mandarin?"

"I was at University, wasn't I?"

"Did you try Xiao or Wu?"

"Nyima tried it. And many variations. Dawa was lucky the thing did not explode."

"Did you try Chien?"

"Of course we tried Chien. We tried everything we could think of."

Mila handed the mapping device back to the mayor. "Try 'Jimmy' for your password," he suggested. "J-I-M-M-Y."

Jamyang the Mayor was not as surprised as Mila thought he would be. He regarded Mila cagily. "Jimmy, you say?"

"That's right."

"And why would you guess Jimmy, right off the top? Eh? I told you the fellow's name. It wasn't Jimmy."

Mila laughed. "Well, Mayor, The soldier had a third name. His friends called him Jimmy."

Jamyang paused thoughtfully. Then, holding the device as far away from him as he could, he typed in JIMM. Positioning his finger over the final letter, he averted his face and squeezed his eyes closed. He typed Y. The device beeped and lighted up its little screen. Jamyang looked up delightedly.

"Come, Mila—how did you know his password?"

Mila did not want to tell the Mayor about his ability to share the mind of another. So he just said, "I met the man before he died." Which was true enough.

Jamyang gave Mila a sharp look. "You were in on it. Why keep it a secret?"

"I was not sure what would happen to the women if I snitched. Besides, I am no informer."

Jamyang was a tolerant man. He clapped Mila gently on the back. Together they examined the map device's small green screen. They could both read the Chinese characters of the main menu:

1. Communications
2. Global Position
3. Tactical
4. Help.

"First, let us make sure that we are not broadcasting our position back to Chinese headquarters," suggested Mila.

Jamyang entered the communications option, confirming for Mila that the transmitter was set to off. The two men familiarized themselves with the other communications options, none of which seemed useful without two or more units. Jamyang then initiated option two, Global Position. It displayed not only current coordinates for the map device—the coordinates of Freetown—but also detailed maps of the surrounding mountains. The men made appreciative noises over the maps. "I do not believe we Tibetans have ever owned one of these before," said Mila.

"Look," cried Jamyang the Mayor, "here it displays the minefields we cross to reach Freetown. Look at these safe corridors, wide as highways." He pointed a quivering finger. "And this way is also safe, as is this way, to the east. If only we had this device three years ago, eh, Mila?"

"Or ten, or twenty. But then the information would no longer be current," said Mila dryly. "We must look on the bright side."

He peered over the Mayor's shoulder to see the map display. "Does it show the mountains behind Narkang Prison?" he asked slowly. "The cursed minefields around the city?"

Jamyang the Mayor fiddled with the controls. "Here is a tactical map of the area around New Tibet City. It shows Narkang here. It shows the positions of the Tactical Areas, that is the minefields, the guard posts, and even the dog runs. Look, it shows terrain. It even differentiates different kinds of concertina wire."

Mila took the unit into his hand and admired it. "Such a clever device," he admitted. He studied the map. "According to this map," he mused aloud, "a man can stay in these northern woods and get very close to the outermost razor wire perimeter of Narkang."

Jamyang frowned and looked over his shoulder. "Yes, you can get very close. But only to the wire. One cannot get through the wire undetected, not even with this device."

"Certainly not." Mila was intimately familiar with barbed wire, since wire and mines were the solution to every Communist security issue. "But there are many ways to salt tea."

Jamyang looked deeply into Mila's face. "I wish you would forget Narkang Prison. You have an unhealthy obsession with the Dalai Lama."

"That much is certain."

"I become exasperated. Mila. Why must you be such a fanatic?"

"I admit that I have been painted with that brush, but I do not even know the definition of fanatic."

Jamyang winked. "One definition you did not learn in school, eh?"

The reference to his philosophical education caused Mila to pause.

"Oh, I can posit the definition of fanatic. Give me a minute."

"No need. A fanatic is a man who is determined to give up

his own life in a doomed attempt to get Tara Gyatso out of prison," said Jamyang sternly.

Mila glared at Jamyang. "That is not true. And besides, that is an illustration, not a definition."

Jamyang laughed. "It's a bloody good definition, too, even without positing and illustrating. And I don't want to see you being a dead example of it."

"I don't plan to be killed, Jamyang. That is why I am so interested in this map thing." Jamyang held up his hand and they both looked at the bulky unit.

"We must ask our expert Nyima to confirm that it is not broadcasting a signal," Jamyang decided. "The enemy would very much like to retrieve this."

He turned away, but Mila stopped him with a hand on his shoulder:

"Jamyang, I worry that with this device you will become the violent scourge of these hills. Then the Chinese would surely hunt you down."

Jamyang paused with a thoughtful expression. "Our future is by no means certain, with or without it," he admitted. "But I can tell you one thing that is certain . . . "

"She will never be released," said Mila, returning to an earlier topic. "That would be the height of folly for them."

"I am afraid you are right, brother," said Jamyang. "They will take no further chances with Tara Gyatso. They will see her imprisoned or dead, but never free."

"One day she will be free."

"Sayeth the fanatic, heh? Still, we must never give up hope. I spend my whole day with foolish hopes. And as you know, cousin, she was born under a lucky sign, forty yojanas high."

Mila smiled. "The white elephant."

"Meanwhile, you and I are free. There is much to be said for that!"

Mila was in agreement with that sentiment. Excepting bears and land mines, there was nothing he dreaded more than prison. He turned again to studying the unit's maps.

Later that night, Mila lay with Dolma on a bed of rushes near the mouth of the cave, an archway onto a black sky full of stars. Mila was healing quickly. Dolma made sure his starved, scarred body was clean and that his wounds were packed with fresh herbs. She rebandaged him daily, a charity to which the entire population of Freetown contributed rags.

Dolma seemed especially quiet and thoughtful. Throughout their dinner and lovemaking, she held a topic in reserve. Now she sat on the ground beside Mila and let him comb her long black hair, a job he did well with only one hand for the comb. They stared up at the unwinking stars.

"Mila, you remember the Chinese soldier we . . . um . . . ."

"I do."

"Today I went up into the hills to revisit his body. I wanted, I needed . . . " She was stalling, unsure how to broach this topic.

"It must have been hard for you to see the body," Mila ventured.

"Oh, it was not so hard. The birds and the crawlers have been at him these weeks, of course, and something larger, too—perhaps a pack of dogs."

"Not my old friend *Dom*?"

"Probably not. *Dom* might bite a living man, my darling—especially one who shouts, 'Hey, go away!'—but he did not eat this dead man's flesh. It is a pack of something smaller, with sharp, eager teeth."

"What did you need with the body?"

"I needed the skull."

"Oh, of course, the skull." *No toadstools and bears around Freetown.*

"Do not think worse of me, Mila. We must have a skull cup

to perform the rituals. This is the perfect skull for three reasons. Would you like to hear what they are?"

"I would, most certainly," said Mila, still combing her long straight hair. "I presume it is in that leather bag you have there."

"There is no hiding anything from you, Mila. Although actually, since you mention the head, I must say there is more of the man still attached to this skull than I need. I will have to cleanse it."

"A nasty job. Are you up for it?"

"I think so. Why not?"

"All right. What are your three reasons?"

"First, this particular skull will be auspicious for your practice of projection because you have already looked out of its eye sockets."

"I see. What is the second reason?"

"It will be auspicious also for *my* practice of projection because I emptied the eyes of life. Since I emptied them of life, the skull is suitable for my own use."

"That sounds like very strong magic."

"It is of the strongest. So you see, we both have a connection to this skull."

"Not a very cheerful connection," observed Mila.

"What skull is cheerful?"

"My own skull is full of cheer. Quite lit up with it, in fact."

"So is mine, now that you mention it."

"What is the third reason for choosing this skull?"

"The third reason is that I did not have to enter a minefield to get this skull, which cannot be said for many skulls in Tibet."

Mila nodded enthusiastically. "By god, that is an excellent reason."

"Also, I would rather do to a soldier's head what I must do to this head tonight. So, that is four good reasons."

"I can understand your feelings, and I submit to your logic," said Mila, returning her brush. "However, I think I will excuse myself from this part of the preparations. I will go out among the people—yes, I feel that strong—and spend some time with Jamyang or the twins while you make all ready."

He wanted to tilt up her chin with his right hand, but he had none, so he reached around with his left hand and tipped her head gently back, kissing her lips. He had wanted just one sweet kiss before he left, to thank her for being such a beautiful witch, with a forehead and cheeks that glowed red in the firelight, but now he found he was aroused. Perhaps it was speaking of the dead—a pastime to make the living feel more passionately alive. Dolma acceded to his lovemaking eagerly, but carefully—he was still very tender in eight separate places.

They were getting better at making love with three arms. When they had finished, Dolma redressed Mila's shoulder and side, which were oozing a clear odorless pus, and Mila went out into the night. The cloudless sky was alight with sparkling stars. A cool breeze refreshed his cheek. This is called happy, he thought with satisfaction. He stopped to commemorate the moment. Happiness so good is rare. May all creatures have it and its causes. And so saying he thought of the lovely Dalai Lama, alone in her cell on this cool night, and he looked up into the sky and prayed for her deliverance. Because of the darkness, he did not see the falcon circling far overhead in the obscure silent night, tracking Mila's every movement; nor did he spy the dread silhouette of *Dom* the bear, hiding in the woods on the upper hillside, sniffing Mila's scent but afraid to venture down into Freetown. And not seeing, Mila went happily to the Mayor's cave for a bowl of *chang*.

8

Weeks passed without incident. To the amazement of all, for the first time in years it snowed. Snow fell steadily all winter, closing the mountain passes around Freetown. For Mila and Dolma, the thick layer of snow outside increased their mutual absorption within. They began sleeping during the day and spending their nights embracing before the warm fire, or practicing the rituals associated with the Projection Yoga.

The soldier's skull was boiled and scrubbed until it was clean and white, the cup sawed off, and the inside painted light blue. Weird blue light leaked through the eye sockets.

The skull was centered on a low table, woven of pine boughs, serving as an altar. Behind the skull were arranged votive candles, flowers, mirrored balls, and incense. In front of the skull were small bowls holding fruit, *arak* wine, and pieces of fried meat, as well as two special bowls of spring water dyed bright yellow with saffron. The saffron water froze during the night, but the magic was not in the water.

Mila and Dolma practiced every night. They knew when the night was too cold for sitting on the damp rock, and they spread straw. The blue skull cup grinned madly out of the cave at the empty sky. The shadows danced on the wall opposite the fire. Mila chanted the rituals and charted the couple's progress toward projection. Dolma was in ecstasy. She told Mila that their meditations were close to bearing fruit. She was sure that soon they would feel the bliss of mutual transposition. Meanwhile, she and her lover remained firmly anchored in their own hearts—as they had every day through the frigid days and freezing nights of snow.

One day the snows ended and blue skies appeared high above the surrounding mountains. Mila strapped on snowshoes plaited from reeds and hiked into the rocky high country atop a crust of snow.

The snows had arrived in late November that year, and although deposits were nothing compared to the thick blankets of the previous century, there was more snow than had been seen in years. Mila rejoiced in the high thin altitude, the bitterly cold air, and the total silence of the woods. Looking out of the trees, he could see across to the opposite range, which rose up out of the tree line in an unbroken wall of snow. Although wary of avalanches, he felt glad to be surrounded by snow mountains.

Mila saw a falcon hovering high above, balanced on its spreading wings, its compact golden body trembling slightly as it rode a thermal updraft. Mila believed he had seen the bird on other occasions, and wondered if it was the very bird he had flown with. Mila felt a pang of envy for the bird's effortless flight and superb view, but mindful of Dolma's warning, he turned his eyes to his snowshoes and trudged slowly up the sharp ridge, cresting the top. At the top it appeared there would be a route home in descending east between two high shoulders of snow upon rock into a narrow valley. He was almost certain the next gap led back to Freetown. After resting briefly, he began his descent without incident and reached the shelter of white-blanketed pine and larch on the lower slope.

He had not gone much farther when he came upon an

animal trap in which some creature—perhaps a monkey—swung in a cage hanging from a tree. Thinking that this was bound to be one of Basang's animal traps, Mila reached up instinctively to free the frightened creature, whereby his clumsy movement triggered the trap, slipping its noose around his wrist and whipping him into the air all in one lightning motion.

Mila dangled by his wrist. A thin cord or wire had pulled its knot firmly into the flesh. The hanging front of each snowshoe could just brush the ground. All of Mila's weight was on his wrist, the knot tightening ever more painfully. This would be an excellent time for another arm, he thought grimly. With a sudden conviction that he was being observed from above, Mila looked convulsively upward around his now agonizing shoulder. Yes. There in the sky was a circling falcon. Feeling a nameless panic, Mila yelled loudly for help.

Mila hollered off and on with increasing desperation and distress until he saw the big bear ambling toward him through the trees. *Kun cho sum!* thought Mila with a terrible shock of recognition. It was old *Dom*.

Dom came casually down the hill, placing one pigeon-toed paw before the last and sinking deeply through the crust with every step. Mila conjured into his mind a quick image of a terrified, tethered sheep, having its first long look at the mountain lion for which it is bait. It seemed a grimly realistic appraisal of his situation.

As the big bear shambled toward Mila, opening his terrible jaws and growling, Mila settled his mind. He imagined he was bathing his injuries in a cold mountain stream. He examined the dislocated shoulder, the stressed arm, the swollen, mottled flesh of his wrist, and the blackening fingers of his unfeeling hand. He tried to visualize the pain as dark discharge into the water. He remembered his own blood flowing red into the water, that day *Dom* bit into his skull. The pain flowed like that, and Mila watched it pour darkly into the cool, clear waters of his empty mind. He held the empty vision as long as he could, but it was hard because the bear was almost upon him. When the bear was so close that Mila could feel its hot breath on his face, Mila snapped back into his pain and abruptly catapulted into the mind of *Dom*.

With a dreadful dislocation, Mila found himself inside the body of the bear, staring into the terror-stricken face of the dangling man. Mila's projection had caught the bear in the very moment of launching his attack, every muscle tensed to deliver a smashing blow with his claws and a terminal bite of his massively strong jaws. Unlike his previous projections—thanks perhaps to his practice of the rituals—Mila found himself in sole possession of the bear's mind. He tried to stop the attack. He relaxed the bear's flexed muscles and let go of the red-hot rage that boiled up his spine.

Mila dropped the bear's body out of its fighting stance and took a pace back. He sat it on its haunches and regarded his own body. Had the projection worked in two directions? Was Mila's body now inhabited by the mind of the bear? Mila leaned forward curiously, instinctively employing his tan snout for the purpose of acquiring information. The harmless-looking biped was foul-smelling in the usual way of men, but as Mila pushed his muzzle closer, the dangling human bear roared with rage and pain and pulled itself nearly chin high on its one dislocated arm, the better to defend itself with its rear paws.

So the bear inhabited his human body. Under duress, Mila had accomplished the yoga of projection. Dolma would be proud, if he could only get the chance to tell her. But like having a dangerous tiger by the tail, Mila had a furious bear by the body. As long as he was inside the bear, he was safe from it. But he could not abandon his own form. He needed the human body. Mila hated to leave it suspended from the tree, but did he have another choice? Probably not. *Dom's* fighting spirit was best left hanging.

"I must go now, bear," Mila growled to the dangling human

form. "Deeply sorry to leave you hanging, but you will be safe in this tree. In any event, if I cannot find a way to get us safely back into our bodies, we will both die in these hills."

Without warning, a ball of fire struck Mila in the shoulder with great force. The sound of a rifle shot echoed across the snowy hills, and every creature in the forest instinctively looked uphill. Mila knew he had been shot. A terrible burning told him it was a slug big enough to kill a large bear. He turned clumsily, looking for his attacker.

Just as the echo of the report boomed from the far ridge, Mila saw the distant form of Basang, the setting sun glinting off his rifle barrel, tracking him inexorably with its telescopic sight. The pain and trauma of the bullet in his back was beginning to scatter his consciousness. He will kill me if I remain in the body of the bear, thought Mila, trying to focus. But if I return to my own body, the bear will die.

With this thought, he was back in his own pain-wracked human form. His arm and shoulder were almost numb, his body freezing cold. Another shot boomed across the mountain ridge. The world spun slowly. There lay the black mound of fur dusted with snow. There were its eyes. There was its blood. *Dom* was dead. The great bear was slain. Mila spun slowly at the end of Basang's trap. He tried to say a prayer for his departed foe, but he could not concentrate. He was ready now for Basang to cut him down. He hoped Basang would hurry. Damned Basang—the slowest and most methodical man in the Himalayas.

Later that night, suffering from a bruised and dislocated shoulder and a lacerated and severely sprained wrist, Mila finally achieved mutual transposition with Dolma. He found himself in the body of his loving consort, gazing down at his deeply etched, ape-like face with amazement. As he gazed, the expression on his battered features rearranged itself into a radiant glow, and he knew his old face was feeling a wealth of unknown emotions.

Still later, when the night had become very cold, Mila awoke and felt the pain in his shoulder and wrist. He remembered being in the bear and he remembered being in Dolma. He had strong feelings for the woman who nursed him and strong feelings for the beast that took his arm. He lay quietly, listening to Dolma's rhythmic breathing.

Later that night Dolma stirred and saw that her man was still awake. "Tell me what hurts," she said, touching his bruised arm.

"It is nothing," said Mila. "The pain is mostly in the water."

9

In Mila's youth, winters had been long and cold. But since he had gotten older, the planet had also aged. The snows failed, the ice melted, and the hot winds of the southern oceans whistled through the arid mountains. Long years passed without snow.

This year the welcome snows had fallen onto the parched, burned, stunted, starving hillsides. Although Mila did not know it, the rains also drenched the grateful plains below.

Even when winter ended, spring rains poured across the Himalayas, swelling the streams with ice-cold rapids. Days and weeks of warm yellow sun carpeted the green hills and hollows in a riot of colorful flowers.

During these beautiful spring days, Mila often accompanied Dolma on her walks into the high valleys. Dolma visited the most remote areas that could be reached on a day's trek. She prowled the hillsides and streams looking for healing plants and herbs. She gathered ginseng, holly root, mountain dragon, and *tianma*. She filled her apron with dangshen root, wormwood herb, and larkspur. Later, Dolma pressed them between moist ferns and put them into leather bags.

"We can sell them for a good price in New Tibet City," she said happily.

"It will be good to see our friends in the city. What do you intend to buy?"

Dolma laughed gaily. "I am thinking to buy some delightful Chinese perfume that I smelled a few years ago. Some chamomile as well."

"I would like to visit my old tent," said Mila with a studied, casual tone. "Perhaps my tools are still there. I could bring them back to Freetown with me."

Dolma looked at him contentedly. She took him by the arm and kissed him.

"These are happy times, aren't they Mila?"

He returned her kiss. "They are happy," he finally conceded.

"It is good to be alive. When will we go to the city?"

"Purbu and Pemba have been scouting for game in the west. They say the rivers are still too high to cross. We cannot leave until the week after *losar* at the earliest."

Dolma gazed dreamily into Mila's gray eyes. "It is not long before *losar*," she said. "I will mend our boots and leggings." She put a finger to her lips. "And the skull needs a touch of paint."

Losar was the Tibetan New Year. Each Tibetan celebrated his or her birthday on *losar*, and it was traditional on that day to feast on *mo-mo* dumplings and *kap-say* cookies and to drink copious amounts of *chang*.

The Freetowners gathered early in the day to prepare the food and drink. They gathered in an open glade near the swift cold creek in the warm afternoon sunshine to share the meal and the happy occasion. All agreed that the *mo-mo* were plentiful and delicious and the *chang* intoxicating. Before anyone became too drunk, Mila suggested prayer for the independence of their nation and the freedom of the Dalai Lama. Dolma excused herself, saying the *chang* had upset her stomach, and expressed a desire to retire to her cave. Mila looked at her with concern, but led the prayers, and with the familiar words he gradually forgot her absence.

After this patriotic interlude, the Freetowners considered themselves free to drink and laugh. The clever twins had whittled a fife and stretched a lyre during the winter. They played a number of hill songs, to the great delight of the men. The flute was sweet and tuned, but in the absence of catgut the lyre's strings were waxed hairs plucked from the longest queues in camp. It did not remain in tune, but the howling music was welcome entertainment.

Mila relaxed at his ease and drank a few cups of *chang*. He was happy to be sitting in the warm spring sunshine with his friends. The faces of the men were shining from rich food and the warmth of pleasurable company. The twins played away happily on their instruments. Basang was in fine voice, singing in an operatic falsetto, and Jamyang the Mayor sat beside Mila. The two men regaled each other loudly with tales of freedom fighters and their brave escapades. The others laughed and sang while some played a game with a plastic platter, skimming it low over the sweet green grass, perturbing the droning honeybees and decapitating the sunny dandelions. Only Nyima frowned and fidgeted with discontent. Mila watched the man for a while and decided that he was either wrestling with his conscience or his bowels. Shortly thereafter, Nyima shot Mila an uneasy look, rose from his spot, and hurried off down the valley.

Mila had another cup of *chang* with the Mayor and launched into a long story about a jolly Catholic priest he had met in Narkang Prison. Remembering just in time the horrible outcome of the priest's incarceration in Tibet, the tipsy Mila quickly invented a happy ending wherein the cleric was airlifted safely back to the Vatican. Jamyang could not credit the tale, but Mila refused to back down, insisting on the impossible denouement as if it had really occurred, even though Mila had been present at the man's terrible death.

"Come, come, Mila. It could not have happened as you say."

But Mila did not want to remember how it actually ended for the sorry priest, and he was trying hard to believe it had happened the way he was telling it. Finally Jamyang had enough, and he stood up angrily, flinging down the rag he had used to wipe grease from his chin. "This story you are trying to tell me is a lie," he exclaimed. "I am surprised at you, Mila. I always thought you were a truthful man, and now you are telling me stories as if I were a child. Airlifted out of Narkang Prison? Bah! Flown in safety to Italy? Pah! What do you take me for, a fool?"

Mila found himself unaccountably angry with the Mayor for refusing to believe his lie.

"I am telling you the damned truth," Mila swore. "You can go to hell if you do not believe me!"

The Mayor stormed off sputtering, leaving Mila to wallow in his own shame. Usually he shunned a lie, but today he had imbibed too much in honor of *losar*, and Mila was a sadly inexperienced drinker.

He stood unsteadily. He felt in an ugly, reproachful mood. He wandered through the festivities without seeing the happy, merry-making groups celebrating the New Year. He did not see Dolma. Then he remembered that she had gone back to their cave. He walked down the valley to see if she could improve his mood.

She was not in the cave.

Maybe she had gone out for a walk in the woods. He felt some anxiety—bears. Then he remembered her bags of pungent herbs. Dolma was probably safe from bears. But where was Dolma?

He was peering myopically into a grove of blossoming trees when he heard the shot. He spun around, his one arm swinging out, an animal sound in his throat.

He ran back to the sound of a shouting crowd: Freetowners hurrying toward one of the cliff's broken faces—the cave of Sonam and Ani-la.

Mila ran. When he reached the cave, Jamyang emerged with

a startled expression. "Do not go in there, Mila," he said. "It is Dolma. She has been shot."

Mila halted. "Dolma shot?" he cried. "How is Dolma shot?"

"It was Nyima." Mila tried to get past him, but Jamyang held him firmly. "Nyima shot her," he repeated. "And she is dead. Do you understand?"

"Dead?" echoed Mila quietly. There was a commotion behind the Mayor. Basang, Purbu, and Pemba emerged from the cave. Basang was holding a long camp knife.

"Nyima stabbed her!" cried Basang, on seeing Mila.

"He raped her!" cried Purbu in distress.

"Well, let's find the bastard and kill him," suggested Pemba, with crazy reasonableness in his eyes. "He hasn't gotten far."

Mila stared, stunned, at the group of men. He looked from one to another: the red-faced Mayor, the emotionally distressed twins, Basang with hatred in his eyes. Everyone was quiet. They looked at Mila. Mila felt hot. His hands were wet.

"I want to see her body," he said.

"Mila . . ." began Jamyang, nervously licking his lips.

"I will see the body. Then we will decide what to do."

With Jamyang preceding him, Mila entered the darkness of the shallow cave. He could see nothing at first, but his senses were alert with the smell of gunpowder and blood. The buzzing of flies had already begun—soon they would be black on the body of the dead woman. He knelt beside her. There was no doubt she was dead. The bullet had killed her immediately. There were wounds from the knife as well. The body lay on its back with arms and legs akimbo. Her clothing was torn and in disarray. Her lovely features were frozen in a death grimace, and her opened eyes bulged unnaturally from the pressure of the bullet's passage. The weapon itself lay where it had fallen beside the blankets.

Mila pressed his fingers over her eyes, trying to close them, but one eye still protruded. He smoothed the black hairs away from her forehead. He adjusted her torn clothing as best he could with one hand, in the forlorn hope of restoring dignity to the corpse. It hurt him to feel this body, a body he knew so well, now lacking all response. Why must the body be so warm? Why must the body be so soft? It smelled like Dolma, but with the accompanying tang of the unwashed rapist.

Mila tried to stand; Jamyang helped him to his feet. Mila swayed unsteadily.

"Jamyang," he said. He gripped the Mayor's arm.

"Yes, my boy?"

"I am sorry I lied to you earlier today."

"You lied?"

"About the Italian priest. He did not escape to Italy."

"Of course not." Jamyang clapped him on the back. "But it has no importance now, my son." They were speaking in undertones. To Mila, the dark cave seemed to be folded in around them, like the stone walls of a prison.

"No," Mila insisted. "I think it does have importance. It seems more important now. Now that Dolma . . . " Mila's mind was drifting, breaking into several streams of grief. But he persisted. "I want to tell you, Mayor. About the priest. There was no happy ending. There was no rescue."

"Of course not. I never entertained the thought."

"Do you want to know how he died?" Mila was crying, the hot tears running down his seamed cheeks.

"Now, Mila . . . " The Mayor placed his hand tenderly on Mila's shoulder.

"They used water, Jamyang, water."

"I am sure it was horrible. Those bastards." The Mayor was patting the distraught Mila on the back.

"Dolma's death was quick, wasn't it Mayor?"

"It was, Mila. It was a mercy."

"But the priest took forever. He took forever to go."

"Poor bastard."

"I loved her, Jamyang."

"You were lucky for a while, dear Mila. Nothing lasts."

"Her death was quick. The priest's was slow."

"I am sorry, Mila. I am sorry about Dolma. I am sorry about the Italian priest as well. He should have stayed in Italy. What more can we say? But now we have important decisions to make. Are you ready? We must go after Nyima, before he gets away."

Mila shuddered, stood straight, and wiped his nose with a dirty sleeve. He gave Dolma's body one last look.

"Let's talk to the men," he suggested

They went back into the light of the New Year.

Basang and the others were slinging rifles and canteens.

"We should not let him get too far ahead," said Basang. "Let's go!"

"What will happen when you find him?" asked Mila.

Basang raised his rifle. "I will deserve a medal from the Nuclear Safety Council." He and his party disappeared into the hills.

The remaining men watched him go. Jamyang wiped his hands on the greasy leather of his pants.

"Now, Mila," he said gently. "We have work to do. Nothing for a one-armed man. You have paid your respects. What more can you do here?"

Mila understood. He turned and left the vicinity of the crime. When he reached the cave he had shared with Dolma, he hesitated. The men were inside, out of sight. Mila hurried across the clearing to Jamyang's cave. He moved aside the old horse blanket that covered the opening. Jamyang's dwelling-place smelled of cold incense and muscle balm. Mila looked around, remembering the Chinese soldier who had died here. Now his killers too were dead.

On the far side of the cave were Jamyang's camp bed and an

old pack holding his meager belongings. A quick glance beneath the straw mattress revealed nothing, but sitting in Jamyang's pack wrapped in his sheepskin vest was the molded plastic device Mila was looking for.

He tucked it into his blouse and left Jamyang's cave.

Now it was late afternoon. There was no one in sight. Mila hurried back to his place and hastily rolled a few necessities inside his bedroll—a canteen of water, a bag of pemmican jerky, a knife. Into his tunic went a wad of writing paper and a biro pen. He slung his pack and added a modest bag containing a grinning skull.

Mila stepped out of the cave in time to hear one distant shot. He stopped and waited. The afternoon sun slanted in a yellow beam across the little valley, illuminating the upper slopes in gold. The weather had grown colder in the west. There were no more gunshots. Basang had needed only one.

That night he traveled westward across the mountain flanks, trying not to lose altitude, watching the moon ascend above the peaks, sometimes descending to walk through wet valleys where raindrops and moonlight glittered in the spiderwebs. Sometimes he climbed above the tree line, traversing high country knee-deep in snow, freezing without his shawl, but never lost, thanks to the plastic device.

When dawn came he was northwest of New Tibet City, at the terminus of a logging trail between two vast minefields stretching away to the north and south, protecting the city's western approach. These were the same minefields that had menaced Jamyang and Mila the previous summer, their outlines clearly visible to Mila on the map device. The day promised to be warm and mild. Having walked all night, Mila prepared a sheltered place: he gathered a bed of reeds and branches, then slept through most of the day. High above, fleecy clouds moved slowly across the empty blue sky, but Mila's dreams were troubled.

Mila arose from his hiding place when the sun was over the

western mountains. He marched confidently during the night, his legs strong from trekking in the snows. He came often to iron-cold streams, swollen by the melting snows, where the temperature of the water made his teeth ache. Later, when the moon rose, he was able to quicken his pace, and by dawn Mila was within ten miles of New Tibet City, traveling a safe corridor between the mines.

He found cover in the deep brush and slept. Just as the previous day, his dreams were troubled. His mind converted the sound of running water into the march of booted feet, and he awoke often during the day.

Night fell. Mila filled his belly with pemmican and cold water and began walking again. The miles went quickly. Mila crossed a dirt track road that might once have been used for military vehicles. He looked at the map device. One sloping arm of a far higher range separated Mila from New Tibet City. On the southern side, a broad forest of conifers concealed Tactical Area One guarding the northern approach.

Mila moved on. He followed the dirt track road before striking out south towards a pass between two rugged scarps. Reaching the top of the pass presented him with a fine view: the twinkling electric lights of downtown New Tibet City, the many campfires glowing among the tents of the Tibetan quarter, and the silent dark bulk that had been the Podrang Palace. Floaters came and went from a large Army garrison far off to the west, and there were headlights moving east on the Highway of Tunnels. He knew exactly where he was, but he calibrated his position on the little glowing screen before continuing downhill. He walked carefully, for the electronic map indicated that death and maiming awaited those who ventured off the narrow path.

Mila descended along what might once have been a well-used smugglers' trail. The going was steep, and from time to time the trail assumed the character of a mere indentation in a rocky cliff, but Mila smelled success now and he hurried on. Within a few hours he came to the edge of the forest. He stood at an artificial tree line beneath which the forest had been sawn down. A hundred meters of stumps led to a tall chain-link fence topped with razor wire, securing the perimeter. Beyond that fence was a run for the military dogs, their genetically altered vision well adapted to hunting in darkness. Finally, far below, stadium lighting illuminated the prison's inner defenses, administrative compound, cellblocks, and yards. According to the map device, the Dalai Lama's cell was somewhere between two thousand and twenty-one hundred yards from here—depending on where she was held within the walls of the prison.

Mila retreated back into the trees until he came to a sheltered bowl of fallen rocks. Mila sat on a flat rock and composed his thoughts. He felt tired, but it was necessary now to write a letter; a letter he had been contemplating as he walked. There was moonlight, there was paper, there was a biro pen. Everything he needed was right there in his tunic.

Mila began writing, using a shorthand *kyuk* script familiar to Tara Gyatso but unlikely to be decipherable if discovered by a passing soldier. He wrote:

To Kundun, Seventeenth Dalai Lama—

Mila paused, licked the nib of his pen, and thought a moment, looking very much the schoolboy.

My dearest Tara,

If you are reading this letter then my plan has worked. Sitting here above Narkang Prison, I have managed to snatch you out through the walls, past the guards, over the wire to this rocky place, my dearest friend, where you sit reading this letter. Also, of course, the reverse has happened. It is now my own unworthy consciousness that inhabits your form. I hope you will forgive me for liberating you in this unorthodox way, without your prior knowledge and consent. I could think of no other method.

Forgive me also for not having taken better care of this body I leave here to you. *Rather stupidly, I lost its right arm—an accident in the woods. I don't miss it much, but now I wish I had been more careful. Please think of this body as a durable beast. Do not pamper it; it is used to hard work.*

Here Mila paused and massaged his left temple with his five fingers, as though a sudden pain had come to him. Then he wrote again:

Look carefully through the pockets of the clothes you are wearing. You will find some items to help you escape back into the hills. In particular, I have left you with a map device. The password is "Jimmy." I have entered the coordinates of a place called Free-town. There you will meet patriots who will aid our cause. They will know you on sight. Ask for one named Jamyang.

In prison I will pretend to be Tara Gyatso as long as I can. You will need some time to organize your plans. Of course, the Tibet-ans must know your identity. From Freetown the word will spread. Even if they suspect me I will tell them nothing—at least for a while. They will not believe in the possibility of transposing two minds—not at first!

Mila paused in his furious scribbling and looked around the sky. The sky was dark, and the moon was low in the west. Soon the heavens would show the violet light of dawn. He wrote one more line:

My dearest Tara, you have been very patient for fifteen years. Forgive me for taking such a terribly long time. I am coming for you tonight.

P.S.—Please do not concern yourself about me. I am used to prison life and I will make out fine.

Mila folded his letter and slid it into the breast of his tunic. He arranged his bundles carefully beside his seat and opened the leather bag containing the polished skull. He detached the skull's cup and set it aside. He pulled his beads from the skull where they lay coiled like a serpent. They rattled across the cold bone.

Starlight filled the empty blue space inside the skull. Mila began chanting the familiar ritual. Mila closed his eyes . . .

When he opened his eyes again, he saw he had been transported to a divine palace. Its walls were translucent green marble veined with gold. They were inlaid with sumptuous jewels and adorned with hundreds of dazzling golden statues. Through the walls he could perceive other areas of the palace, vast halls populated with magnificent and grotesque beings, radiating light. The air was scented with incense, and the music of a thousand lyres thrummed delightfully in his ears. He was seated on a magnificent throne covered with luxurious furs. An attentive and respectful retinue of devas and bodhisattvas stood admiringly on all sides, their palms pressed together in prayer. Mila looked down at his body. It was elegant and graceful, beautiful and youthful. More divine than human—and startlingly green—it radiated clear light from within its skin. His elegant garments were woven from adamantine threads and embroidered with complex designs. A garland of blossoms gave out their sweet smell. His feelings were of pure bliss, and his mind was focused one-pointedly on the meaning of reality. Mila had never felt so wonderful. He had not expected this divine transformation. He realized immediately that he had entered a mandala created through the power of Tara Gyatso's mind; an imagined world, a perfect visualization she had created out of nothing from within a union of calm abiding and special insight. It did not exist in actuality but was the appearance of her meditative state. Mila's transposition with the Dalai Lama had occurred while she was absorbed in this trance of exquisite beauty—a trance so thorough and profound that even sliding his own impure consciousness into its mere imprint was a sublime and convincing experience.

Still, he knew that his mind was not the powerful agent of visualization that had created this mandala. He could not sustain its lovely proportions and perfect detail. Even as he knew this he felt the stability of the visualization decrease, saw the colors become less vibrant, heard the music less harmoniously, and felt a sharp pang of hunger in his green belly. Gradually, but quickly, the visualization faded. The magnificent golden walls lost their luster. The light that radiated from his body became dim. The garland of flowers wilted and the scent of sandalwood turned stale. The sounds of music began to seem like cries of despair. The retinue of devas and bodhisattvas holding offering chalices collapsed into a swarm of vermin drinking water from a tin bowl. The jeweled ornaments that surrounded him resolved into piles of straw. His throne was a meager palette of dry husks, and the smell of incense was the sour reek of human sweat. The walls of the palace were covered in grime and black mold. The golden floor was sodden stone, only dimly perceivable in the absence of light. The feeling of bliss in his body was missing, now replaced with the familiar ache of hunger, bruised ribs, freezing feet, and itching scalp. He felt the sting of open sores on arms and legs. His nostrils filled with the smell of prison.

He was home.

10

Mila's prison day began before dawn. Rolling the thin nun's cloak into a ball, he sat cross-legged upon it, ankles cold under a sheaf of pale yellow straw. He meditated, as usual, visualizing Tara's green-marble mandala, but without her startling clarity. Often his mind wandered. He considered needful things: the care and feeding of the Dalai Lama's body; the sorry condition of her bowels. He measured the strength in her arms and flexed the arthritic knee. How had she injured that knee? He imagined Tara Gyatso free, in the sunshine, recruiting partisans. A one-armed man with two good knees.

On the offensive . . .

Mila wondered when Tara Gyatso had become a nun. There had been rumors, of course, but no confirmation of her ordination. It shook him at first. Luckily, Mila had studied the monastic curriculum and was familiar with the many rules of monkhood. Nuns committed to these same rules and eight more besides, which Tara Gyatso had once assured him were designed by men. Mila did not remember what they were, but he was probably less likely to meet a monk here in the women's isolation block than in any other place on earth, so it did not really matter. But from the first, he made strong efforts to live within the discipline, not least because monastic routines are ideally suited to prison life.

She did not have a mirror and he longed to see her face. He could feel with his fingers that it was sunken and seamed; her once aristocratic nose had been broken long ago and was flattened off-center. Each month, after head shaving, he ran the hair that fell onto the prison stones through his fingers. Black mixed with gray. What he could see of her body was depressing, yellow with prison pallor and plagued with the unhealed sores of prison nutrition. It sorrowed him to be able to count all twelve pairs of ribs.

The red and yellow robes of her lineage—donated by the other nuns, her prison *sangha*—were aged and patched. The thin fabric was no protection against the sharp straws of her pallet, resulting in a backside ignominiously, but painfully, pocked.

His first month behind the walls: Mila crouches in a bar of sunlight, listening carefully to the quiet stillness of the cellblock, the clanging of doors, the staccato foot patrols. The numbing routine of an isolation block.

His second month behind the walls: Mila stands day and night staring out the window. On those rare occasions when he sleeps, he has a recurring dream. In his dream, Tara Gyatso sits wearily astride a shaggy horse. She is not in Mila's old, battered body but in Tara Gyatso's more appropriate female form. She wears white. On some nights she looks peaceful and radiant but worn, as if fasting. In others, she seems determined not to cry. In all of Mila's dreams, she is making her plans, gathering her forces, making speeches. Dreaming and awake, crouching in the sunbeam, staring out the window, Mila nurtures his hope.

His third month behind the walls: Mila begins each morning with meditation, but some mornings his faith is shallow, his motivation is negative, and the mandala manifests only vaguely. After his meditations he stands looking pensively out at the ruins of the Podrang Palace. Her eyes are sharp, but his thoughts are muddied.

After four months behind the walls, Mila felt he had grown into his prison role. Gradually he had come to understand that he had three goals: deception, ethics, and physical health. Maintaining the deception was vital; it would give Tara Gyatso time to organize her forces. The ethics were simple: the monastic discipline. Maintaining physical health was the hardest. A method for keeping her ailing body healthy was not immediately obvious. Seeing her chronic malnutrition, he adopted a strict regimen for improved health: prison food and prostrations every day after meals, pale face held up to the afternoon sun for vitamin D.

The prison food was of poor quality, consisting mainly of rice gruel and orange *dal*. Mila knew from his own experience that a prisoner's diet is designed to be deadly. Scurvy loosens the teeth. Malnutrition weakens the bones and the will. Older prisoners are pathetic skeletons; they do not have the will to live. But Mila was determined to put a pound of flesh on the Dalai Lama's frame. He made this resolution each morning as the morning meal was brought to his cell. Green broth, rice, and tea. The tea was served in a brown ceramic pot. The military guards stood silently while he ate. No one remarked on the Dalai Lama's newfound appetite.

More months went by.

Some mornings—always following the departure of the two guards—the Assistant Warden would make a visit to the cell of the Dalai Lama. His name was Zhang Zhi Rong. Rong was a pompous career man who hoped some day to be head of corrections in one of the eastern provinces, or even in the capital. He was a pervert who liked to confide to Tara Gyatso his sexual exploits among the women prisoners, speaking in graphic detail of his twisted encounters, writhing with pleasure as he did so. But he never directly admitted to these acts of sadism. Instead, he played an unpleasant game with Tara Gyatso called "What Would Be the Karma If?"

This was such a morning. Following the departure of the

two guards, Assistant Warden Zhang Zhi Rong arrived at the door of the Dalai Lama's cell. "Ah, my dear Dalai Lama," began Rong, seating himself on a chair brought in by one of his attendants. "I hope you are in good health today."

"Very good, thank you," agreed Mila. They spoke in Chinese.

"No recurrence of the old pelvic problem?"

Mila was in fact concerned with some persistent pains and stiffness—he suspected rape—but he was not about to involve Rong.

"No problems at all, thank you, Warden."

"I could authorize a pelvic examination. We could get that troublesome pelvis looked at."

"You are kind, Warden. I have no health problems at the moment, thank you. I will let you know the moment a problem occurs."

"Of course, of course." Rong looked disappointed. He was a pathetic man, and might have been a harmless deviate, except for his power over the female prisoners. He rubbed his chubby hands.

"You know, Dalai Lama, I always enjoy our discussions about religion." He paused.

"As do I, Warden." Mila answered warily.

"Of course, as I have explained to you, religion is an antiquated and false system. It has no validity in the modern world. The Party tolerates religion just as we tolerate other minority behaviors, but eventually it will die out."

"You have kindly explained this to me before, Warden."

"There is no ultimate truth other than the Communist Party. You understand that by now, do you not, Dalai Lama?"

"I try, Warden, but it is difficult for me to understand these complex matters."

"I see that, but I am unsure why. Your Buddhist religious beliefs are fairly complicated, are they not?"

"Certainly, and they are also very difficult for me to understand."

"I especially enjoy thinking about your outmoded system of values you call cause and effect."

"We have had many interesting conversations about this topic, Warden. Wouldn't you like to discuss something else?"

"No, this interests me. For instance, what would be the karma if someone falsely accused and then imprisoned a young woman because he was hotly attracted to her youthful charms? Eh?"

"I am not exactly sure, Warden," sighed Mila. "It would be negative, in any case."

"And what would be the karma if he kept this young woman under his observation, day and night?"

"Again, the karma would be negative, Warden. But, surely, no man would stoop this low to satisfy his pleasure?"

"Certainly not, certainly not." The Warden mopped his sweating brow. "This is just a hypothetical discussion of religion. But what would be the karma, Dalai Lama? According to your outmoded system of thought? What would be the precise effect from indulging in gratifications such as these?"

"The precise effects of actions are very hidden from us, Warden. I cannot tell you. It would all depend on the severity of her sufferings, their length, the number of incidents involved, your intentions, and so forth. Still, from the hypothetical case you describe here, the effect would be very negative. Rebirth in a situation of similar injustice would be the best one might expect, I imagine."

Warden Rong considered this, wringing his hands anxiously.

"I see, Dalai Lama. Now tell me this: what would be the karma if this young woman had a sister . . ."

Mila was spared the details of this further confession by the opening of the iron door to his cell. The same attendant who had brought Rong's chair now entered and whispered urgently in his ear. Mila could not hear the whisper, but the startled response was louder.

"What?" said Rong. "He is here? You mean now?"

The attendant nodded gravely and whispered more of his message. Rong frowned deeply, glanced at the Dalai Lama, and stood to take his leave.

"Something has come up, Dalai Lama. I must leave you now. Please prepare yourself for a visit from General Cheng Jia-ming."

Mila looked at Rong carefully. They both knew that General Cheng Jia-ming was a frequent visitor to Tara Gyatso's cell. Something else was wrong.

"Perhaps he wishes to play chess," suggested Mila to Rong, as he turned to make his exit. It was a plausible suggestion. Chess was a tradition between the two old adversaries. Mila had been surprised the first time the General stopped in for chess. In fact, since Mila had been in Tara Gyatso's place, the General took chess with his famous prisoner once or twice each month. This might have proved awkward, except for the fortunate circumstance that it had been Mila himself who taught the Dalai Lama the game.

The Warden looked back at her with eyes that were pouched in purple flesh. He licked his lips quickly, snake-like.

"Perhaps a hypothetical discussion of politics," he said. "I hear he is furious, fuming, in a foul mood. But you will see the General soon, Dalai Lama. Let me know if you need special medical attention following his visit." He fled the cell, footsteps echoing down the stone corridor. Then silence. Mila could hear the blood rushing through his ears. It was perhaps not good that General Cheng Jia-ming was coming.

The General was a venerable, gray-bearded warrior in his seventies, tall and thin, with drooping brown eyes and condescending lips. He commanded the Army garrison in New Tibet City, an important provincial command. The General had a youthful new wife in Beijing and three boys in private school in Taiwan.

Mila assumed General Cheng Jia-ming was obsessed with Tara Gyatso. Mila had him pegged as dangerous and passionate, ruthless and cruel. As Mila suspected, General Cheng had once demanded sexual favors from his famous prisoner. But all Mila knew for sure was that the Dalai Lama and the General played chess in her cell, and sometimes the General spoke to her nostalgically and a little suggestively about times "neither of us can ever forget."

On those days when he desired a game of chess, the General arrived at Narkang Prison with a military escort. He himself carried the ivory inlayed chessboard, clasped under his arm against the thick, crisp wool of his tailored uniform. The enlisted men placed the table and chairs and arranged the pieces on the board. From other hints the General made, it appeared that Tara Gyatso refused to play white and that she usually won with black.

On this hot summer day, the cell was like an oven. Mila was nervous. He feared detection. Nevertheless, the usual ritual was carried out. The General entered the cell and was greeted by the seated nun. His men set up the table and arranged the pieces, all according to established custom. The General stood by in an attitude of parade rest. His wizened face did not appear furious. To Mila he seemed relaxed and under control. But the General was a man whose thoughts were difficult to know.

The enlisted men saluted and left the small cell.

"Well, Tara, I hope I find you well," said General Cheng Jia-ming, pulling out a folding chair and sitting opposite to her.

"Thank you, General; I could not be in better health."

"I am glad to hear that, because it seems to me you have been somewhat troubled these past months."

"Troubled? Not at all, General. I thank you for your concern, however." Mila remained wary.

"In some ways it seems to me as if you are a different person."

"The General is a student of human nature."

"Even your chess seems different. You are far less tactical in your play."

"I am striving for a more positional game."

"Far less aggressive."

"I have grown too old for the attack."

The General laughed dryly. "I would like to believe that," he said.

They began their game. The General was an aggressive player but not patient enough to array his forces well. He led his pieces in a doomed assault against Mila's strong defenses, after which the counterattack swept him from the board. They played another game with the same result. Mila sometimes wondered if the General had led soldiers into battle in the same reckless fashion.

"Checkmate in two," announced Mila.

General Cheng Jia-ming scowled at the board.

"This is what I mean," he said angrily. "Suddenly you play chess like an old woman. You sneak around behind your defenses. You prey on weakness."

Mila said nothing. The General lit a small brown cigar, as he often did. It gave off an acrid and unpleasant smell that lingered in the air for hours. He composed his features.

"Tara, I need to speak with you about something."

"Certainly, General."

"There is a disturbing rumor flying around this city. The rumor speaks of a freedom movement growing in the hills, led by a one-armed renegade."

"A one-armed renegade? That is a disturbing rumor."

"It is exceedingly disturbing."

"Why exceedingly? Surely a few Tibetans and a one-armed man are no threat to the People's Army?"

"Certainly not . . . as long as you are here in prison where I can keep an eye on you."

"That is a compliment, I suppose."

The General regarded his cigar. "Yes," he said dryly, blowing on the ember. He blew an elegant circle of smoke into the still, dim air of the cell.

"They say this one-armed man is named Mila," the General continued. "I find that odd. I recall that you had a friend named Mila. He was arrested with you in the uprising of '99 and released last year. He was political, but harmless. I myself interceded in his behalf, sparing him the firing squad. Could this be the same person?"

"Probably not. The Mila I knew was, as you say, harmless. Also, he had two arms."

"Come, lady. A man may lose an arm."

The Dalai Lama's shoulders shrugged. "Mila is a common enough name. The fellow I knew is timid. Not at all brave. He is inert. You have some other Mila on your hands, General."

The General blew smoke languidly across the chess table. His eyes glittered unnaturally, and Mila wondered if he was taking a drug.

"My spies also say another thing. They say it is widely rumored within the Tibetan community that you and this man have switched bodies. They say Tara Gyatso is the one-armed man. They seem to think that *you* are the person named Mila. They tell me all of Tibet believes that you have returned the Dalai Lama to them. They are rallying in support of this crazy, senseless idea."

Mila laughed in a way that he hoped was realistic. "Switched bodies? Do they say how we managed that marvelous trick?"

"You know as well as I that such magic is a feature of Tibetan legend."

"Of legend, certainly," said Mila carefully. "But surely no one believes it is possible in the real world?"

"What is the possibility?" asked the General, never taking his eyes off Tara's face.

"General, Communist doctrine holds that mind and matter are one. How could a material mind be projected to another body?"

"Do not spout Communist doctrine to me, Tara Gyatso. We both know there are more realities than those contained within Communist doctrine."

Mila saw that the General was furious.

"General, do you actually believe this absurd rumor?"

"I do *not* believe absurd rumors! However, I do suspect something. I suspect that you, Tara Gyatso, are once again engaged in activism. I have no proof of this, of course. The guards' reports are inconclusive. This troubles me. I am determined to get to the bottom of it. I will have to subject you to tests."

"Subject me to tests? General, I live a quiet life. What do the guards report?"

"They say you have started eating rice. You have not eaten rice since '04. You have even gained a little weight. I am told by the Warden you have put on half a kilo. So. What am I to think? You are marshalling your strength. You are playing chess the way Mao waged war. You are engaged in some sort of political activity. I see all the signs."

"That is ridiculous!"

"Do not presume, madam, to call me ridiculous!"

There was a long, angry pause.

"What sort of tests?" Mila finally asked.

"I want you to have a loyalty test, Dalai Lama. Then I will be satisfied. A good old-fashioned loyalty test, yes? When was your last one? Can you remember?"

Oh, yes, Mila remembered. He had been subjected to many loyalty tests over the years. They involved, among other things, freezing cold showers and electric shock. The loyalty test instruments recorded everything. Brain activity, blood pressure, adrenal levels, electrocardiogram, chemical levels in the organs, tensioning and cramping in muscle groups—but especially the sharp spikes in neural activity as the current was supplied. It was all logged in the mainframes. Loyalty tests were conducted within defined parameters.

Tara's proud head did not move. "I have done nothing and do not require a loyalty test."

The General stood and bowed. "Nevertheless, I order it, along with a complete search of your quarters. Do not worry. It is quite all right. We are a country of laws, you know. You will have the right to remain silent."

Mila stood as well.

"Until the next time we meet then, my dear **Kundun**."

"Thank you for the games of chess, General."

General Cheng Jia-ming clapped his hands, summoning his aides. Within a few seconds all evidence of his visit was gone, except for the dampening effect of his baleful glance on exit and the lingering reek of tobacco.

The sun was high in the sky, and the temperature in the cell was stifling, when the clang of the iron cell door roused Mila from his morose introspection.

They marched to the hospital.

The hospital was in the southeast corner of the complex: a sterile-looking building with windows made of glass brick reinforced with stout iron bars. The roof of the hospital was fringed with razor wire and each corner was surmounted with a guard tower. The walk across the baking asphalt courtyard was long and painful. The asphalt was soft beneath the hot sun.

The sunless interior of the ancient hospital smelled cold. Dead cold air circulated in a whisper from the ventilating ducts. The entry hall tiles were cold underfoot. On the walls were murals from the time of Mao. They depicted historical scenes: Mao swimming the river in shades of blue, a famous dinner party on Mao's birthday. Tara was led past the murals to the front desk. A prim nurse rose to her feet to meet the famous prisoner. She was late.

The nurse had been waiting. No need to apologize. She would now ring for Assistant Warden Rong as instructed. Please have a chair. No chairs? The guards waited in silence until the hospital doors opened. They saluted Warden Rong. A young woman doctor came through the swinging doors from the emergency reception area. Warden Rong introduced Dr. Poochi to the Dalai Lama. The Doctor smiled and took the Dalai Lama's hand. She examined it clinically, turning back the long fingers, testing the musculature, pinching the fingers together. "Does that hurt?" she asked.

"Yes."

Dr. Poochi, the Warden, and their famous patient walked the hospital corridors. Dr. Poochi expressed her admiration for the Dalai Lama and offered to serve as her personal physician during her incarceration as well as "after her happy release." Mila thanked her graciously. She was a young and pretty woman, with long black hair, lively eyes, and sharp teeth.

The trio arrived in a laboratory situated not far from an exterior wall. It was large. Digital readouts, oscilloscopes, printers, and equipment consoles lined the wall. Security cameras monitored the laboratory. In the middle of the room, an old-fashioned medical chair was bolted to the floor. It boasted stout restraining straps lined with sheep's wool. Dr. Poochi seated Mila in the chair. There were eight straps. Two secured each arm and wrist, a thick strap was tight around Mila's waist, the head was immobilized. Each ankle was bound to a chair leg. The sheep's wool was not soft at all, but coarse as if repeatedly soaked in brine. Mila flexed his fingers. He licked his lips.

Dr. Poochi settled a tiara of electrodes onto Mila's shaven head. She connected the device to a machine that stood nearby.

"These electrodes will record any stress you may feel during today's loyalty tests," said Dr. Poochi brightly, pulling on some latex gloves. "They simply record your systemic responses. Just relax, Dalai Lama. There is nothing you need to do. If you speak, please tell the truth. Also, remaining silent is your right. Although you have the right to remain silent, we appreciate your cooperation. We will give a little and take a little, all right? Everything will happen quite naturally. I am very experienced with all of this equipment."

The doctor reached into the pocket of her lab coat for a sheaf of paper forms. "Warden, we can get this paperwork out of the way?"

Dr. Poochi and the Warden bent to their papers for a few moments. During that time, Mila flexed his fingers and tried to calm his mind. He remembered his painful times in the hills, especially with the bear. He remembered losing his arm. He remembered how he left his body to avoid the operation. He wished he could he do that now, avoiding the unpleasant business unfolding around him. But he could not risk leaving Tara Gyatso's body.

Suddenly Dr. Poochi was standing next to the chair. Had they already concluded their paper work? Mila's mind must have wandered. Dr. Poochi flicked a switch on the nearest console. The device began to hum.

"I commend you, Doctor," put in Warden Rong. "Today's loyalty test is being carried out in a most clinical and professional atmosphere."

"I thank you, Warden," beamed Dr. Poochi. "I pride myself on keeping the equipment in perfect order."

"What would be the karma, Dalai Lama," asked the Warden, "if we performed the loyalty test in an unprofessional manner?"

Mila did not answer. He needed a calm mind. In Narkang it went without saying, his right to remain silent was going to be painfully earned . . .

. . . until the guards unstrapped Tara Gyatso's body and lifted her from the chair. Mila was soaking wet. Dr. Poochi wrapped an ace bandage tightly around her patient's fingers.

"The patient remained uncooperative throughout," reported

Dr. Poochi with a frown. "I employed all sanctioned inducements without success. I recommend seeking permission for expanding sanctioned inducements to include truth drugs."

Warden Rong agreed. "I will seek permission from the General," he assured the Doctor.

"Good. Then perhaps it will be my pleasure to see you again tomorrow, Dalai Lama?"

Mila could say nothing. He found to his surprise that with the help of the guards he could stand. He wondered if the search of his cell had been completed. He did not think they would find anything interesting. He needed to lie down on his pallet of straw.

Outside the hospital building, Mila relished the yellow sunlight on his upturned face. Mila was glad to be out of the cold hospital and in the sunshine. It was late afternoon. At least the entire day had not been lost to torture. The afternoon sun was hot. The soft asphalt stuck to his bare feet. The courtyard was loud with the clanking of chains. All prisoners in the hospital and administration buildings were being escorted back to the cells. Mila's short walk seemed to take a long time. At last he was at his cell door. Mila had a sudden, frightening vision of a gaping iron door opening onto hell, but it passed. No need for nightmares. The cell itself was hell enough. The guards locked the door behind him. Mila crawled to his pallet. Getting as comfortable as he could, Mila catalogued his injuries. The main of these were broken fingers wrapped tightly in an ace bandage. His wrists and ankles were bruised and sprained. His back had been wrenched against the straps. His ribs and spine were sadly bruised, but no ribs appeared broken. He had not been given a mouthpiece, and his teeth had chattered. His tongue was bitten and his head went round and round.

Got off easy, he reflected, feeling a loose tooth with his tongue.

Mila dozed. When he awoke it was still late afternoon. The

cell was hot, the walls radiating heat. Fleas hopped wildly in and out of the straw. Raising himself carefully from the floor, Mila moved slowly, painfully, to the bucket of water. He felt old and spent. One eye was blurred and there was a ringing in his ears. He felt a little better after drinking. He rinsed and spat out the coppery taste of blood. Moistening a cloth, he gently bathed his face. His left hand was badly swollen. The ace bandage was much too tight.

Feeling better after washing up, Mila stood without caution. Sudden movement; loss of balance; weak knees; his vision blurred. Mila reached an arm out for support. He pressed his sweating palms into the stone. He leaned his head against the wall. The stone was cool against his forehead. He heard a strange rhythmic rumbling. Opening his eyes, he stared at the texture of the stone until his vision cleared. Then he pulled himself up to look out the window.

The city was kilometers away, but he could see it well enough from this height. A huge crowd had assembled—a giant demonstration that must have begun while he was in the hospital. The city was swarming with crowds. Tibetans streamed out of the encampment, climbing the hill to the Podrang. Thousands were making their way to the top. Tens of thousands filled the blocks around its base. Hundreds of thousands crowded New Tibet City, waving the red and yellow flag of Tibetan independence.

From time to time the crowd cheered wildly. A great shout went up from its collective throat. Something eventful was taking place at the very highest point of the Palace. Those on the slopes surged toward the summit.

On the very summit stood a familiar figure dressed in white robes. Mila could not see him clearly. He stood in the midst of a group of men struggling with a rolled banner. He pointed dramatically down the western slope of the Palace. From Mila's vantage point he appeared to have only one arm.

The men on the Podrang suddenly loosed the banner. A vast canvas sheet unfurled partway down the steep side of the building. It stuck. Some of the men carried long forked sticks. They prodded the bundle until it rolled free. Mila smiled. The banner was huge. He could easily read it. The whole world could read it.

We Still Live.

Author's Note

The Tibet of *She Still Lives* is purely fictional: it is not meant to be the real Tibet. Similarly, the people and religions of New Tibet City are not to be confused with actual Tibetan people, their religions, and their future. But even though New Tibet City and its brave inhabitants do not exist in reality, compassion and nonviolence can be found just within: more powerful than weapons of war.

Bill Magee
Dharma Drum Mountain, Taiwan